Dreamer

Ballerina

From the Chicken House

When I watch football my FEET copy the moves, and Sarah Rubin's clever, inspiring story made my feet want to DANCE! It really doesn't matter what you look like, or where you come from, it's the magic of movement INSIDE that makes the difference. I loved reading about Casey – and I was there with her every dance step of the way.

Barry Cunningham
Publisher

Dreamer Ballerina

Sarah Rubin

Chicken House

2 Palmer Street, Frome, Somerset BA11 1DS
www.doublecluck.com.

Text © Sarah Rubin 2011

First published in Great Britain in 2011
The Chicken House
2 Palmer Street
Frome, Somerset BA11 1DS
United Kingdom
www.doublecluck.com

Sarah Rubin has asserted her rights under the Copyright, Designs and Patents Act, 1988,
to be identified as the author of this work.

Cover illustration by Nila Aye
Cover and interior design by Steve Wells
Typeset by Dorchester Typesetting Group Ltd
Printed and bound in Great Britain by CPI Bookmarque, Croydon, CR0 4TD

The paper used in this Chicken House book is made from wood grown in
sustainable forests.

1 3 5 7 9 10 8 6 4 2

British Library Cataloguing in Publication data available.

ISBN 978-1-906427-61-0

For Chris

Chapter One

Rat-a-tat-tat, my feet hit the ground, and the sound sings up like music. I am dancing on the sidewalk, skipping home from school, free as a bird, and my feet are flying. People stare then look away fast, but I don't stop dancing. Not for them, not for no one.

With small, soft steps, I glide over the ground, kicking up dust in little red clouds around my toes. Dangling from its strap, my school bag bangs against my legs as I go. I can feel Miss Priss and her posse behind me, walking to Vicky's Ballet Studio for their class. They're all sweater sets and saddle shoes, but I know they've got pink tights and pink leotards and pretty pink satin ballet slippers in their bags, locked up tight against the red, South Carolina dust.

'Hey, Bigfoot!' Miss Priss yells. 'Have you ever tried walking? You know, like a normal person?'

I stop dancing and turn slowly on the heel of my left foot. Miss Priss only moved to Warren two months ago. She already thinks she's the Queen, just 'cause she came from stuck-up old Greenville. Just 'cause she's been taking ballet lessons since she could walk. The air is hot and dry, and the sidewalk seems to crackle and shimmer in the heat. We haven't had the rains yet, and the dry grass crunches under my shoe as I turn. I pretend it's Miss Priss.

'No,' I say. 'Have you?' And I enjoy watching the flush spread up across her face like it's a smear of Carolina dirt on her clean white shirt.

'You are so weird.' It's the best she can do, and I smile because I know my weirdness offends her. My weirdness has power.

My right foot comes oh-so-slowly to stand beside my left foot. Then I start swaying – hop to the left, hop to the right. My one-two-step power dance.

I am spinning and swaying on the sidewalk in front of Vicky's Ballet Studio. Everyone can see, driving by in their shiny new Cadillac cars. A group of high school boys drives past in a beat-up Ford truck, their hair slicked back and glistening with grease. They yell and whistle as they go by, but I don't care. I am flying high, dancing free under the clear blue sky. I leap like nothing can hold me down. Miss Priss just stares in horror, her face all red because she's been seen with me. I've got her now. My arms go up in the air as I let out a joyful whoop. And then I lose it.

The sound of my voice breaks the spell, and the other girls start to laugh. They crow and cackle and feast on my mistake. Miss Priss raises one bony finger and points at me. She shrieks with laughter, forcing it out until she doubles over, gasping for air.

Now it is my turn to blush. Hot, shameful flames lick up the side of my face. I try to keep dancing like I just don't care. *I don't care.* Miss Priss laughs like an ugly monkey, so who cares if she's laughing at me?

But my feet get tangled. My left foot hooks on the back of my right shoe, and down I go into a heap. One messy pile of arms and elbows, legs and skinned knees.

'Looks like you have two left feet, Bigfoot,' Sally says.

Beth howls, 'You mean two left bigfeet!'

They all shriek again even though it's not funny. It isn't even clever. Then, Miss Priss stands up straight, and carefully smoothes her hand over her ballet bun.

'I can't believe you think you can dance. You are the worst dancer I've ever seen.' She sniffs, brushing down her skirt. 'You have no technique whatsoever.'

The other girls sniff too. Sucking up to their new Queen Bee. And then, without another word, they stick up their noses and walk into Vicky's Ballet Studio, leaving me sitting in the dirt alone.

I want to scream and shout, but I can't. I'm too angry to speak, and being angry makes my eyes fill with tears. I bite my lip hard to keep them back. She should be the one sitting in the dirt, not me.

I can feel the people on the sidewalk looking at me, and the people in the cars driving past. And I know what they're looking at, too.

They're looking at my skinny chicken legs poking up from the ground, and my scrawny arms that are all elbowy. And they're looking at my ratty-tatty, used-to-be-white, two-sizes-too-big, Converse high-top shoes. They're saying, *That Casey Quinn is an awkward child. She ain't got no grace, and she ain't no beauty neither.*

It's true my nose is too wide, and I'm freckled from head to tappin' toe. Even under my hair I'm freckled. And maybe my ears do stick out like two mug handles, but I do have grace. I have more grace in my pinkie toe than I bet you've ever even imagined. I have more grace in my left little fingernail than new-to-school Miss Priss Ann-Lee and all those pinky-pink ballet girls put together.

I take a deep breath and stand up, brushing the dirt off

my skirt as best I can. I hear the piano music coming from Vicky's Ballet Studio. I take a quick look behind me, step off the sidewalk, and snake around the back of the building.

I drop my school bag by the base of the low dogwood tree, and scramble up the branches, my heart trilling to the music. I climb up three branches, until I can see in the back window of the studio.

They're all dressed in pink now, and standing at the bar that's bolted to the wall. I watch as they bend and straighten their knees, and then lift their legs high in front of them, toes curved into perfect points. My bones ache to dance along. But I don't move a muscle. I just watch Miss Vicky with my eyes wide open, 'cause if I blink I might miss something.

I don't take ballet lessons. We don't have money for extras, and Miss Vicky doesn't give lessons for free. And even if she did, where would I get ballet slippers? Miss Priss's hand-me-downs? I'd rather give up gravy than take charity from that toad.

So I don't take lessons from Miss Vicky, but I don't need to. I practice every morning. Dancing the sun up out of his bed with my long legs and pointed toes. And I've checked out every book on ballet in the Warren County Library so many times they are practically mine.

Besides, this is 1959, not the 1800s. We've got washing machines and power-steering. You can get on an airplane and go around the world all the way to China, where they eat with sticks instead of forks. And there are even rockets that can shoot to the moon. Anything is possible. That's why my great-great-granddaddy came to America. He sailed all the way over the Atlantic Ocean from Ireland. He had a dream, just like me. So he came to the country where dreams come true.

My great-great-granddaddy came to America to make his fortune. He came close, too. He had his own corner shop in New York City, but he gave it all up to marry my great-great-grandmother. He moved to Warren to help run her daddy's farm. My gran thinks that it was real romantic, but I think it was just plain foolish. Why would anyone want to come to Warren? Maybe it was OK back when there was farming, but not anymore. Now it's just dusty roads that go nowhere, and people who stay in one place. You can read out the course of your life if you're born in Warren, as plain as if it was already written down in a book. I want more than that. I want things to happen in my life – big things.

My dream is to be a dancer. Not just any dancer, but a real star. Ever since I was a little girl I've been dancing. My gran took me to see the ballet when I was small. We saw

Cinderella, and I can still remember the feel of the red velvet seats against the back of my legs, and the sound of the audience humming with anticipation. And then the curtains opened and it was magic. The dancers, like music notes come to life, were graceful and strong. My legs kicked and my toes pointed, and I wanted to scramble down the aisle and dance with them. And right from that moment I knew I had to be a ballerina. I was born dancing, a true-blue sky dancer. And I never stop.

I dance my way home from school. Fast and hard on angry days, my feet biting the sidewalk like mad dogs. Long and slow when I'm sad. And every-which-way when I'm glad. My feet become drums as they *slap, slap, slap* on the sidewalk. Stompin' soles with stompin' soul, and nobody can tell me to turn them down.

And I don't *need* music to dance, but when I hear music my feet are fire – not hot, but kicking like the flames themselves. Reaching down into the ground, then up into the sky, in my high-tops I fly when I hear music.

So maybe I don't have no pretty pink satin ballet slippers. But can *you* kick the sun to help him up in the morning? Can *you* jump up and touch the moon? Can *you* dance with the stars in your hands?

I can.

The music changes inside Vicky's, and the dancers

move into the center of the room. They stand perfectly still and then, suddenly, they're spinning up onto one pointed toe and whirling round in tight little circles. My toes twitch as I watch, and I scoot further down the branch to get closer to the window. The leaves and heavy white flowers shiver and shake around me as I move forward. I can hear the branch creaking, but I just hold my breath and shuffle closer. I need to see what they're doing.

I am clinging like a cat to the very end of the branch, just out of reach of the window. It's open just a crack to let the air in, and the music is twirling up out of the gap. Miss Vicky's in the middle of the room. She stands statue still with one leg behind her and one arm in front, and then UP. She is spinning on her front leg, back leg bent up like a flamingo. Miss Priss and her ballet bunch try, and wobble like unwound tops. But I could do it, I just know it.

Snap.

A sound like thunder fills the sky. Before I can look round to see what is happening, I am on the ground. Sitting in the dirt for the second time today. Covered in leaves and giant white dogwood petals. And aching all over.

My head is spinning, but I can still wiggle all my fingers and toes. I sit still for a while, waiting to see if anyone heard me fall. But no one comes running.

I stay still until I hear the music from inside the studio stop, and then I know I need to scoot, or Miss Priss and the ballet bunch will see me sitting in the dirt. I get up slow and bent over. My backside is aching, and when I walk I waddle, but I don't care. I have a new move to try.

I am sore and walking too slow, and it isn't long at all before I hear giggling behind me. I turn on the heel of my foot, wince hard and try to hide it.

Miss Priss and her pinky-pink posse are walking behind me, their eyes lit up like it's Christmas as they huddle around a piece of paper. I don't want them to see me, but I can't move quick enough to get away.

Miss Priss looks up and wrinkles her nose at me. 'What happened to you? Fall over your feet again?'

She and the others are back in their street clothes. I look down. I'm covered in dirt and leaves. I can feel my face going red.

'She's been practicing her "dancing",' Sally sneers, and Beth giggles. I hate their staring eyes.

'Oh, poor Casey. She thinks she's a dancer. Why don't you show us what you can do?' Miss Priss crosses her arms, and all three of them watch me with greedy beady eyes.

I stand up as straight as my sore legs will let me. 'I'm better than you.' Miss Priss is too stuck-up to dance. All she can do is a peacock prance.

She takes a step forward, and so do I. We are toe to toe. Hers splayed out like a duck; mine pointing straight forward like I mean business.

'Prove it,' she says, and jams a folded piece of paper into my face.

It takes a moment for my eyes to adjust. Then I read it: 'The School of American Ballet, New York City. Open Audition.'

'I'm auditioning,' Miss Priss sneers, giving me the greasy eyeball. 'And I'll bet I get in and you don't.'

I take the paper in my hands, gently, afraid it might crumble. New York City – I can hardly believe my eyes.

'What's the matter? Scared?' Miss Priss says.

'Ann-Lee, that's not fair. You know she can't afford to go to New York. They don't even own a car.' Beth pretends to whisper, but I reckon she wants me to hear all the same. And even if I didn't hear, it doesn't matter. I'd know what they're thinking. Everybody in this two-bit town is thinking the same thing. *That Casey Quinn is an unfortunate child: no money, no father, no nothing.* But they don't know a thing. I am not, you hear me, not going to wind up cleaning the hospital like my mama and my gran. I'm gonna get out of Warren, no matter what.

Miss Priss zaps me with her cold blue eyes. Then she turns away. 'Come on. It's starting to smell around here,' she says to the ballet bunch. 'It's just as well Bigfoot can't afford to go. This way she can keep on dreaming she's a dancer.'

They walk past me, bumping my legs with their bags, noses in the air like I really do smell.

I am alone in the hot April sun. My fingers crunch the audition notice. I don't let the tears prick at my eyes until I am sure they are gone. I won't let Miss Priss see how close she got to my secret.

I know I don't look like a ballerina, not in these dirty high-tops with my scabby knees. But inside there is a ballerina leaping to get out, leaping so hard that sometimes I think she'll bruise my heart.

I look at the audition notice again. I don't even care about proving Miss Priss wrong. Not much anyway. If I could only get to the audition, I know I could get in. I have been dancing since the day I was born. But New York City is so far away. There are whole states between South Carolina and New York. I'll bet New York City makes Warren look like an anthill. In a city like that, no one would know where you came from, no one would know you were poor or your father was dead. In a city like that, I could be anyone I wanted to be and no one would laugh at me for trying.

I glare at the street and the cars and the whole two-bit town. Then I shuffle down the sidewalk, past Willy's General Store and the Shell Station, down past where the sidewalk ends. I walk through the oak tunnel with its great leafy branches that throw dapples on the dirt. Toward home.

And as I go, my shuffling gets lighter and lighter until I am floating *gracefully* like a bit of dandelion fluff on the breeze. I am dancing hopeful. I don't need ballet lessons to get out of Warren. I've got my feet. The audition is in two weeks – plenty of time to get a job and earn the fare for the Greyhound. Me and my feet are gonna dance ourselves all the way to New York City. You just see if we don't.

Chapter Two

I don't set the table without being asked. I'm not stupid. That would be a dead giveaway that I want something. And it's no good to let Mama know that. But I do set the table the first time Mama asks. I do a good job of it, too. Three plates that just about match, and cups without chips. Knives and forks squared away.

'Fried chicken?' I ask as I sniff the air. It smells of grease and flour – delicious.

Mama drops a piece of chicken into the pan, and it sizzles – *yessssss*. I lay out paper towels on a plate for Mama to drain the chicken on when it's done.

'It sure smells good,' I say.

Mama turns her what-are-you-up-to eye on me. I hop away quick before she can read the whole answer on my face. It does smell good, though. Mama's the best cook this side of the Savannah, except for Gran, of course. I'd take her fried chicken over fancy frozen dinners on a TV tray any day.

'I'll go get Gran,' I say, and bound out of the kitchen like a cat on a hot tin roof. You can't fool my mama, not for two seconds. I'm not ready to tell her about the audition yet. I need my secret weapon. I need Gran.

She is sitting in her flowered armchair, which is all worn bare with the shape of Gran, feet propped up on an old milk crate painted brown to match the room. Gran works in the hospital mopping floors. Standing up all day makes her ankles swell like the Savannah River in the rainy season.

'Supper-time, Gran,' I say. Gran puts her finger to her lips and shushes me. She is listening to the radio, her eyes half closed as a soft, sticky voice says, 'Oh, darling, I love you.' Then the music starts playing all sappy, and I stick out my tongue and gag. Gran smiles at me and turns off the radio with a sigh.

'Someday you won't pull that face,' she says, but I don't think so. Gran's gooey radio makes my stomach green queasy.

Gran uses her arms to heave herself up out of the armchair. They wobble as she huffs and puffs. You'd never guess it, but when Gran was younger she was Warren's Cakewalk Queen, skinny with legs long enough to reach the sky. Everybody knew my gran, and she won every cake-walk she ever danced in, which is probably why she's so big now. You can't eat that many cakes without gaining weight.

Gran finally gets up with a 'woo' and looks at me. 'You're up to something, Casey. You're twitching like an ash leaf in September.'

She's right. My whole body is lit up and jangling. My fingers go *snap-snap*. My toes go up and down as I balance on my heels. I'm so ready for New York City that my body is already starting to audition. Little kicks and low dips saying, *Watch out, world, here I come!*

'Don't tell me now, save it for the table,' says Gran.

Mama serves me with a plonk of mashed potatoes that looks like the mountains of snow they get up north. Gran's plonk is smaller, more like the snow we get here in South Carolina – which is hardly any at all. She gives Mama 'The Look', but Mama ignores it. Gran is supposed to be minding her figure.

'How was your day, Casey?' Mama asks.

I wrap my tongue around a bite of potato. 'Good,' I say. Then I swallow hard. 'I want to get a job.'

'What?' says Gran. 'Don't be silly, girl. You're still in

school.'

Mama just looks at me. I can tell she's thinking. She's trying to read my face and figure me out. I go innocent with my eyes.

'An after-school job, Gran.'

'What for?' says Mama.

'I want to earn some money.' I say. *Tappity-tap* go my toes under the table, giving me away.

'What for?' says Mama again, her voice heavy as a rain cloud.

I pull the folded audition notice out of my pocket and slide it across the table. The kitchen goes quiet. I don't dare look up. It's getting dark out now. The shooflies bang one-two-three against the screen door, trying to get in to the light.

Mama picks up the paper in her strong, long fingers and reads it. Her lips press into a tight frown, and I stop tapping my toes on the floor – I just wiggle them around the space at the end of my shoes.

Mama passes the paper to Gran. 'Casey,' she says, 'we don't have the money for a fancy ballet school, you know that. We don't even have the money for Vicky's.'

'That's why I want to get a job,' I say.

'Casey, you can't earn that much money in just two weeks.'

Gran finds her glasses and slides them into place. And I watch her with hopeful eyes, 'cause if I watch Gran thinking *yes*, then maybe I won't hear Mama saying *no*.

'I know, but if I do good . . .'

'If I do well,' says Mama. She's annoyed with me.

'If I do well,' I say, 'they'll give me a scholarship. And I know I'll do well. I just need to earn the bus fare to New York City.'

New. York. City. The words trip off my tongue like magic beans. I think it must be the most beautiful thing I've ever said.

'Well,' says Gran, folding the audition slip and handing it back to me. 'That seems fair.'

Now it's Mama's turn to give Gran 'The Look', and it's Gran's turn to ignore it right back.

Gran is the best person in the whole world. I love my mama, but she's serious. She's always trying to nail my two feet to the floor to prepare me for the real world, to make me earthbound. If Gran says, 'Reach for the stars – that way, if you miss, you'll land on the moon', then Mama says, 'If you spend all your time reaching for the stars, don't come crying to me when you walk right into a tree.' She doesn't understand, not like Gran.

I gotta reach for the stars. If I spent my time looking where I was going, all I would see is no-good, nothing-ever-happens, no-one-ever-changes Warren.

'Please, Mama,' I say with big eyes. 'I'll work hard. I promise. And if I get in, they have really good schools in New York, and I could go to museums . . .'

My fingers dance over the table like the corps de ballet, and as Mama watches me, her face goes soft. Mama knows how much I want to be a dancer, and how I practice every morning. I just need a chance, and this is it.

'Please?' I just whisper it now, the ballet shining so bright in my eyes I know Mama can see it.

Mama is quiet for a moment. Then she sighs heavy and smiles.

'I swear, Casey. You could convince a rock to roll uphill if you wanted to. I'll ask Mr Crampton about any extra work that needs doing at the hospital.'

My heart falls down to the bottom of my feet. The hospital?

I remember one day when I was eight years old. Mama had come home from the hospital all wrung out like a wet rag. Her hands red and raw. She looked at me and said, 'You work hard at school, Casey, you work harder than everyone, or else someday you'll end up cleaning the hospital just like me.'

I didn't cry right then. I'm not a big crier. I didn't even cry when we got the notice that my father died over in

Korea. That doesn't really count, though, as I was only two and I didn't really know about him, or the Korean War. But later that night, after Mama put me to bed, I thought about Gran's swollen ankles and Mama's aching back. I didn't want to be scrubbed thin like Mama. And I cried then. I cried and I promised myself that I would never, never work at the hospital. So how can I work there now?

I am about to say no, thank you very much. Then I think about New York City. My heart crawls back up into my chest, beating like a soldier's drum.

New. York. City. Beat. Beat. Beat. I gotta get there, no matter what.

Click go my teeth as I close my jaw. I won't wind up mopping hospital floors for the rest of my life. But if I can earn my bus fare working at the hospital for two weeks, then I have to work there for two weeks. It isn't breaking my promise to myself, not really.

'OK, Mama,' I say. Then, 'Thank you, Mama', when she gives me a stare.

'You can come by tomorrow after school, and I'll see you started.'

'Well, that's settled,' says Gran. 'You can give the patients a recital, Casey.'

Mama frowns. 'If she's gonna work at the hospital, she

needs to work.' She looks at me. 'No capering around.'

I start to nod my head to show her how serious I am, but Gran interrupts.

'Nonsense. She can work and dance, too. It'll be good for those people to see someone lively. Now, pass me the gravy and another drumstick.'

Mama doesn't move.

'Caroline, I said pass the gravy.'

I know Gran is angry now, and Mama's face goes hard when Gran says her name. They always fight about food. And Gran always wins.

Gran reaches across the table and gets the gravy herself. I try my best to sit still so I don't upset Mama more. She can't get mad at Gran out loud, but she can get mad at me.

I hold every muscle tight against my bones, but inside my head I am leaping up and over the table, past the gravy and through the ceiling. I am leaping all the way out of Warren, straight to New York City.

Chapter Three

At school, I feel like I am floating on a secret pillow of air. Everything around me is very far away, and all I can think is, *New York City*. My toes tap under the desk in a rapid *pitter-pat* of steps, as I watch the rest of the class come in from the playground. I never stay outside. Not with Miss Priss holding court under the monkey bars while all the girls come to kiss her feet. But not me. I'd rather sit in a snake pit.

I cross my arms and put my head down on my desk, feeling the cool laminated wood against my cheek.

Mr Richards walks in, but he ignores me. I'm not a grade A student so he doesn't waste his time on me. *That poor Casey Quinn*, he thinks, his eyes swimming like fish behind his big black glasses, *she's none too bright*. Well, maybe

I'm not, but I'll be bigger than he'll ever be. I'll be dancing with the stars before he can count to ten. I smile now.
I'm on my way to audition for The School of American
Ballet. My heart flutters every time I think of it, hopping
in my chest like a jackrabbit.

The late bell rings and the doors open wide. I can hear
the hall flooding with the sound of students rushing in to
find their desks. Stamping and laughing, and the clattering of lunchboxes against the floor.

Miss Priss walks past my desk and stops for a moment,
wrinkling her nose again like she smells something bad.
She was in fine form this morning, all twirling and girly
in a new dress. Her father must be back from another big
business trip. She's always bragging about the presents he
brings back for her: a china doll from New Orleans, pearl
earrings from Little Rock, and now a new designer dress
from somewhere up north.

'Do you smell that?' she whispers to Beth, who is her
favorite today.

Beth and Sally giggle as Miss Priss lifts her feet, one
then the other, checking under her saddle shoes.

'Nothing on my feet,' she says all snotty and stuck-up.
'It must be someone else.'

She looks around the room with big cow eyes and then
smiles at me. I don't look at her. We might be poor, but I

do not stink. I feel a growl forming in the back of my throat, and I glare at the top of my desk.

Miss Priss looks at Beth and Sally, smirking, then leans close to my ear.

'What's the matter, Bigfoot? Can't you afford soap?'

My eyes shoot up, and I wish they could pierce her like tissue. I wish the bomb would land on her fat head and vaporize her so that all that was left were her two stupid shoes. How dare she call me poor? How dare she sniff at me like I'm something stuck in the gutter? I glare at her hard, and she glares right back. We're like two cowboys at high noon, each waiting for the other to draw.

'All right, everyone,' Mr Richards says from the front of the room. 'Go to your seats.'

Miss Priss sniffs one last time. I refuse to flinch. I just stare at her as she slinks away, pretending like she's won. My eyes are hot and dry.

The intercom crackles to life as Principal Haydon comes on for the Pledge of Allegiance. Seats scuff the floor as everyone stands. I watch Miss Priss go all prim and proper with her hand over her heart. Then I look up at the flag, limp stripes of red and white, the blue corner hidden by the folds. Principal Haydon starts us off, and the rest of our voices blend together.

I pledge allegiance to the flag of the United States of America, and to the republic for which it stands: one nation, under God, indivisible, with liberty and justice for all.

Some of the boys at the back of the room snigger; they've made up their own words, but none of them are brave enough to say them out loud. Mr Richards would have their hide. When we're done, Principal Haydon turns off the intercom, and Mr Richards tells us to take our seats.

Mr Richards isn't old, but he looks tired and moves slow, as if his whole body hurts. He wears thick, black-framed glasses like Buddy Holly, but he isn't cool at all.

We all open our history books to page 253. I open mine, but I don't read along. I can't concentrate. Miss Priss thinks she's better than the whole world, but she's not. She's nothing but a toad. I grind my teeth as I remember her snarky face daring me to go to the audition. I'll show her. I'm a better dancer than she'll ever be. And when I think about dancing, Miss Priss slips away. My head is full of whirling images, me in New York City standing on a stage, people smiling and applauding, a bouquet of roses.

I can almost hear the music, a huge orchestra like Gran sometimes listens to on the radio, with all the strings and everything. And there I am dancing, the prima ballerina, long arms and full of grace. My legs stretch through the air as I leap higher and higher, impossibly high as the audience gasps with amazement, and I curtsey . . .

'Casey!'

I crash out of the air sharply and back into the class-room. Everyone is looking at me, waiting for something.

'Pay attention, Miss Quinn,' Mr Richards says in his creaky old voice. He takes off his glasses and cleans them slowly with the end of his tie. Two angry red marks stare at me from where the glasses pinch his nose. 'We're on page 255 now. Please read.'

I look down at my book and shuffle through the pages quickly. I can feel everyone waiting, holding their breath. It seems like forever before I find the right page, my face redder and redder as they watch. Finally I find it. My voice squeaks a bit as I begin to read. Miss Priss sniggers quietly two rows over, but I can hear her just fine. I grit my teeth and keep reading. My stomach quivers like a raw egg.

I finish the page just as the lunch bell rings and every-one scrambles out of their desks, pulling their lunchboxes out and lining up by the classroom door.

Mr Richards looks at me, and I know I'll have to stay behind. He wants to have a talk. I put my head down and shuffle the books on my desk, trying to look busy. When I peek up with one eye, Mr Richards has gone to open the cafeteria doors. I get up and scoot to the back of the line, my brown bag clutched tight against my chest.

But as we march down the hall, Mr Richards is there next to me. He puts his hand on my shoulder, and we stop.

'Casey,' he says, 'you need to stop daydreaming in class. If you don't start applying yourself, I'll have to call your mother in for a conference.'

I nod hard. I don't want him calling Mama. She wants me to work hard in school more than anything, work hard and be smart so I don't end up cleaning floors for a living like her. She'd never let me go to New York if she knew that dreaming about it got me in trouble at school.

Mr Richards looks at me hard, like I'm the history book. His eyes are baggy at the edges, and I wonder what makes him so tired. Maybe me. He sighs again, like he's doing me a big favor.

'All right, Casey, I'll give you another chance, but try to apply yourself a little harder. You've only got one more semester before high school, you know. You need to get your grades up so you can start on the right track.'

I nod. And Mr Richards gets a look like he's just saved the world. I want to roll my eyes, but I don't want him to call Mama, so I hold it in until he turns around. Then I stick out my tongue at his back and turn on one heel to march myself into the cafeteria.

Mama has packed me leftovers from last night, and I

hold them tight to my chest. I don't care if I can't afford hot lunch. Mama is a better cook then those cafeteria ladies by miles.

I square my shoulders and walk into the room, past long tables full of boys trying to make each other snort milk out their noses, and girls giggling about the boys. The air is hot with cooking food and laughter, the other kids talking about *The Lone Ranger* or squeezing around a brightly colored comic. Girls giggling over the pictures of boys in *Teen Parade*. No one looks at me as I walk past, no one but Miss Priss.

She's sitting at the edge of the table, eyeballing me. Sally and Beth sit with her, like two bad shadows. I turn up my nose and walk past. I won't waste my time being sniffed at by a pig.

I see it out of the corner of my eye, snaking toward me, but it's too late. Miss Priss's foot wedges in front of me, and I fall, hard, landing on my brown bag lunch. Potato and fried chicken squeeze out against my chest. Miss Priss laughs. I can feel the cafeteria going quiet, and then a dull roar fills my ears. They are all laughing.

I bite my lip to keep my eyes dry as I stand up. I turn on my toes and face Miss Priss. I can feel my front greasy with food but I don't care. I won't let her see me upset. Not now, not ever.

'Aw, poor baby,' she sings. 'You fell down.'

Beth and Sally giggle behind their hands, but I just glare at them.

'Maybe you should take some dance lessons,' Miss Priss hisses. She is all pretty on the outside, but inside she is rotten. I want to tear out her hair and claw out her eyes, but I don't. I don't do anything. I stand there for a minute, and then I run.

I run hard and fast and away. I just want to be out of that room, with the clattering trays and the echoing laughs. All the faces twisted into horrible open-mouthed sneers. How dare she trip me up? How dare she treat me like I'm no better than dirt?

I rush outside into the sun. The playground is empty. I want to scream my hate into the silence. I gulp at the air, and slam my feet into the ground, stomping and twirling and letting out all the rage. They're still in there laughing, but I don't care.

I wipe my eyes angrily with the back of my hand. And then I sit on my own, my back wedged tight against the school wall, and eat what is left of my lunch. When the other kids come out for recess, I go inside to the bath-room, and scrub at my white dress until it is as clean as it will get. Then I sit alone in one of the stalls, and wait for it to dry.

Chapter Four

I take a long time lacing up my high-tops after school. I don't want Miss Priss and the ballet bunch to see me take the road to the hospital. I want her to be surprised when she shows up to audition and they say, 'We're sorry. We already found our next prima ballerina, one Miss Casey Quinn.' I imagine the green look on her face, and smile. Then I sashay outside, turning my toes toward the hospital.

All around me the other kids are scattering. Some rush down to the athletics field to pick sides for a baseball game; others skip past me toward town where they'll sit at McFarland's counter and sip a soda pop. Gran took me there for a treat on my birthday once. I loved the mint-green plastic counter and the silver barstools that swiveled. The pop was sweet and sticky, but the fizz seemed to burn my throat and made my insides go all jibber-jab.

I float down the street, building speed as I go. I turn right at the station, toward the hospital not the dirt road home. My feet pound the sidewalk all the way. Rapping out a rhythm like excited drums. I'm on my way to work, on my way to money, on my way to The School of American Ballet. I rush past men mowing their old, dry lawns. They try to make them neat and green with bottles of Miracle-Gro, and spray their hedges using metal cans, to keep away the greenfly.

The houses all look the same here, not like down the dirt road where Mama, Gran and I live. Little white boxes, with little green squares of lawn in front, and white picket fences that stretch along the sidewalk. I run my fingers along the fences and feel the *rat-a-tat-a-tat* pattern vibrate up my arm. I don't think I'd like all this sameness. How can you be yourself when you look just like everyone else?

I move faster until the houses are a blur and the fence moves past like the white dotted lines on the road out of town. I race around corners until I can see the hospital, a big red building made of old brick. I'm up the steps two at a time, the sun shining warm against my back. Then I take a deep breath and go inside.

The hospital looks clean, with white tile floors that

make my heels go click, click, click with crisp echoes. But it smells stale and sticky, like an old slice of cheese left too long in the sun. You can tell they've tried to scrub the smell away. That's what Gran and Mama do all day, but the cheese smell is still there. It makes the air horrible to breathe.

I strut myself up to the front desk, bringing my knees up high with my hands on my hips. I ask for my mama. The lady at the desk points me down a long white hallway and some steps to the janitor's office.

'Hi, Mama,' I say. She's standing over the industrial sink, pouring out a bucket of soupy brown mop-water. Gran is drinking a cup of coffee with her feet propped on an upside-down bucket.

'Hi, Gran.'

The janitor's office smells better than the rest of the hospital, like starched laundry and bleach. I wish I could stay here, but Mama hands me a broom and a navy-blue smock.

'You're in the recovery ward, Casey. You need to sweep all the rooms and empty the trashcans into the big bin at the end of the hall.'

I nod. I'm not excited, but I'm ready. I'll get in, get out and get to New York City. No heap of hospital dirt is going to stand in my way.

'It should only take a few hours if you don't dawdle. When you're done, come back here.'

I nod again and turn to walk out the door, but Mama stops me.

'Casey, just so you know,' she says as she scrubs down the sink, 'today doesn't count toward your salary.'

My mouth hangs open as I spin to look at her.

'That's not fair!' I say.

They can't ask me to work for nothing. That's not right. Mama keeps her back to me, scrubbing hard at the sink.

'Didn't you explain?' I ask. 'I need to earn the bus fare for the audition.'

Gran interrupts me. 'Today is your trial, Casey. Think of this as an audition, too.'

Mama flicks the dirty water off her fingers and turns to look at me, toweling her hands on the edge of her smock. 'Mr Crampton doesn't usually hire cleaners as young as you, but I told him you were a good worker. A very good worker. I put my reputation on the line to get you this job, Casey. So you go upstairs and show him I was right.' She puts her hands on her hips for that last bit. 'Now stop wasting time. The recovery ward is at the top of the stairs on the left.'

I am about to say something else. Ask her to explain to Mr Crampton how important it is to pay me. But the look on Mama's face says *hush!* Gran's face says it, too. So I drop my shoulders, and shut my mouth. Then I walk out of the room to find the recovery ward.

The smock is too big for me. It covers up my little white shift-dress completely. I have to wrap the tie around my waist three times just to keep it tight. The pockets that are supposed to be at my middle are closer to the floor.

I can't believe I'm not going to get paid for my work today. I wiggle out the sums in my head, but I'm no good at math without scratch paper. I stop trying when I get to the recovery ward.

It is bigger than I expected. It's a whole floor. Room after room to sweep, with two trashcans in each room. Machines beep and tick and hum, filling the air with technical beats. I step into the first room.

It looks clean already, but this is a test. Mr Crampton will probably come in wearing a white glove, and rub his finger along the floor to see how well I've done. He sounds like that sort of man. I start to sweep. There is a woman in the bed. She's asleep, and I feel weird as I push the broom under her bed, like I'm interrupting her. She doesn't wake up, though.

She is hooked up to a small beeping box, and I start moving in time to the beat. *Beep sweep, beep sweep.* Adding a double sweep every few beeps to be interesting. Before I know it, the room is done.

I take the two trashcans and glide down the hall to the big bin. As I move, the scrunched-up smock around my waist becomes a tutu, and I take tiny steps as if I am walking on my toes. It takes me a while to think of what the trashcans could be, but then I decide that they are baskets of flowers. If I ignore the smell, I can almost see roses.

The next room goes faster now that I've found the beat. I twirl as I push the broom, every now and then stopping to point my toes high into the air as I bend low to pick up a large bit of trash from the floor. It isn't just *beep sweep* anymore. It's *beep sweep leap!* I am the prima ballerina of the recovery ward.

I enter the last room and take a grand curtsey before the bed. One knee bends and the other leg sweeps behind, as I hold up my smock like a dainty skirt. I'm still nose to the ground when a high, whiney voice claws at me.

'Who are you?'

I stand up and suddenly the stage is gone. I'm just a freckled girl with big ears standing in a hospital room and holding a broom. I don't know what to say. A man is staring at me. He extends a long finger and presses a blue button on the side of his bed. His lips curl up at the sides like peeling paint.

'I'm Casey Quinn,' I finally say. 'The new cleaning lady.'

I don't like this man looking at me like I'm just some smear on the floor.

He eyes me and smacks his lips together. 'Not anymore you aren't.'

Suddenly, a gleaming white nurse appears in the doorway. 'What seems to be the problem, Mr Homes?' she asks. Her voice reminds me of Mama's when I ask too many questions.

'This child.' He rubs his hands together like a bug. 'This child has been bounding about the halls, disturbing my rest.'

I take a good look at Mr Homes. He has a round, unfriendly face and glasses that make his eyes enormous. And those enormous eyes are sparkling with glee. He doesn't look like he needs any rest. He looks like he needs a spanking.

'Alright, Mr Homes,' says the nurse. Then she looks at me. 'Come with me, young lady.'

Mr Homes grins, and I hate his evil teeth. I bet he wasn't asleep at all. He was just sitting like a spider, waiting for someone to complain about.

I follow the nurse down the hall to the large white counter. My skin is thick with worry. She sits on one side. I stand with my broom on the other. Before she can fire me, I start to explain.

'I'm sorry,' I say. 'I was dancing to the beeps because I'm practicing to audition for The School of American Ballet. I was being quiet. I didn't mean to wake him up. Please don't tell Mr Crampton, because I need to earn enough money for the bus ticket. I'll be quieter, even though I was being pretty quiet. It will be good practice. Ballerinas are supposed to be quiet.' I stop speaking when I run out of air.

The nurse looks at me. I can tell what she's thinking. She's looking at the too-big smock cinched around my waist and my too-big shoes flopping on my feet, and she's thinking, *This child is no ballerina.*

I try my best to stand up tall and graceful, but it's hard with a broom in your hand. Then her face goes soft.

'Well,' she says, 'Mr Homes is a very particular patient. So next time, no dancing in his room.'

She pinches her lips around the word *particular*, and I know she really wants to say that he is *difficult* or even *rude*, but she's too polite. She smiles at me.

'Do you understand?' she asks.

I nod vigorously and look up with earnest eyes.

'Good,' she says with a smile. I can feel my body going warm and tingly with relief. I like this nurse. Nurse Ryder. Her name seems familiar, like I've heard it before. A bell goes off in my brain. But I'm too happy to listen. Nurse

Ryder is letting me stay. She has soft blue eyes and butter-yellow hair under her nurse cap. And she has a soft face. She knows what's what.

'Well then, go finish your job.'

I turn to go, but she stops me.

'What was your name again, dear?'

'Casey Quinn,' I say.

'Oh, you're in my daughter's class at school,' she says.

I can feel something stirring in the back of my mind. A tiny seed of something very, very bad.

Nurse Ryder just smiles at me. 'I didn't know you took ballet, too.'

I look at her soft face and blue eyes, and then at her blonde hair pulled back in a low bun. She doesn't have to tell me who her daughter is, because, in an instant, I know. I know as sure as I know the sun's gonna come up every morning and shine on my pillow.

I am working for Miss Priss's mother.

And by tomorrow, Miss Priss will know everything.

Chapter Five

I am sitting in my room thinking about what happened at the hospital. I grind my teeth and scrunch up my face. *Stomp, stomp* go my feet on the floor.

I flop backwards onto my bed and look up at the sky. It isn't really a sky, it's a ceiling, but it looks like a sky. Mama painted it for me when I was a baby. She painted the whole room. It's the best thing she's ever done for me. Mama doesn't paint anymore. She says she doesn't have time. But my room is something real special.

One wall is painted like a forest, with thick trees going up to the ceiling. Then the forest fades into a meadow full of flowers, which wraps around the wall. On the other side are a beach and a giant blue lake that sits below my windows. The water looks so real that sometimes, when the sun shines into my room, I really think I'm there. I can hear the water brushing up onto the sand, even though I've never seen a lake in my life. I may only have one pair of shoes, but inside my room I have the whole world.

But none of that is making me feel better tonight. Mama told me Mr Crampton said I could have the job. That should have made me happy. But all I can think of is that Mrs Ryder knows I'm working at the hospital, and she knows I'm going to audition for the ballet. She'll tell Miss Priss, and once Miss Priss knows . . . I don't even want to think about the things she'll say.

Something bad is growing underneath the place where my dinner is. I roll over on my belly to try and squash it. I am not going to let anyone make me feel bad, especially not stupid, stuck-up, I'm-too-special-for-the-world Miss Priss Ann-Lee. I shove my face into my pillow to block out the laughing picture of her snarky face.

She is probably sitting at home trying to think up the best way to put me down. I push my head deeper into the pillow, and bite the thin cotton until I can taste feather. I don't care. So what if I'm working at the hospital? So what if we're poor? My father died fighting for America. What did Miss Priss's father do? Probably nothing. So she can't say anything to me.

But when I wake up in the morning, the thing in my

stomach is still there. It's like an evil worm lurking in my middle, waiting for something bad to happen.

'How come you didn't tell me Ann-Lee's mother worked at the hospital?' I ask Mama.

'They've lived here for months now, Casey. I thought you knew.' Mama reaches forward and takes two strips of bacon off Gran's plate while Gran is up pouring coffee. 'Does it matter?' she asks me.

'It doesn't really,' I say as I munch my own bacon strip. It tastes stale. I can't explain about Miss Priss. Mama would tell me to ignore her. But how can you ignore someone you know is going to be evil to you?

Mama makes me my lunch for school. She packs everything carefully into a brown paper sack. It reminds me of Miss Priss all over again, but I don't say anything. While her back is turned, Gran winks at me and sneaks three slices of bacon back. Gran always wins.

I leave late for school and walk slowly. The closer I get, the bigger the bad feeling in the bottom of my belly grows. It's a giant worm of worry, munching up all of my good feelings like I crunch up bacon. I go past the Shell Station, past Willy's General Store, and Vicky's Ballet Studio. As my feet go slower, my heart goes faster, drumming rat-a-tat-tat with dread. By the time I get to the schoolyard, my ears are so full of drumming, I can hardly hear.

The school bell rings sharp. I shake myself. Miss Priss ain't worth the dirt between my toes, so why am I going so slow? I square my shoulders and march up the school steps. The hall is empty and my feet echo as they slap across the linoleum, but I don't slow down. I am a rocket shooting up to space and no one had better get in my way. Not Miss Priss, not anyone.

I burst through the classroom door and stop fast. I can hear Principal Haydon saying the Pledge of Allegiance through the intercom. The whole class turns to stare, but all I see is Miss Priss. Miss Priss wearing a smile like a fox eyeballing a lame chicken. She just about licks her lips. I can see a large brown bag tucked underneath her chair. It's too big to be a lunch bag, and Miss Priss is far too stuck-up to pack her own food.

'Take your seat, Casey,' says Mr Richmond.

I make my face go fierce, and scoot to my desk. I won't let her see me worry. We finish the Pledge and Mr Richmond starts the class. Part of me goes all limp with relief, but the worm knows something horribly juicy is coming its way. It roils and writhes in my middle. I try to concentrate, but all I can see is that brown paper bag. Somehow I know there is something for me in there. And I know it ain't no slice of rhubarb pie.

As the clock ticks toward lunchtime, I sit at my desk.

I'm staring straight ahead, not looking left and not looking right, like that will keep Miss Priss from coming over. Like if I can't see her, she will disappear. Mr Richmond is scratching out long division on the blackboard, but I can't concentrate. The sound of the chalk seems to squeak out a message. *She's waiting, she's waiting*, it says. I scrunch up my face and stop listening.

The bell rings again at lunchtime. Everyone shuffles their papers and books around me. I keep staring forward. My eyes are on that board like glue and nothing can make me look away, but the worm inside is waiting. Mr Richmond goes out into the hall to open the cafeteria doors. Out of the corner of my eye, I see a pink shape slinking closer. And then Miss Priss is there standing right in front of me.

'My mother says you're working at the hospital cleaning floors after school.' She says it sweetly but loud. She wants everyone to listen. They do, too. They pretend not to notice, but the rest of the class stops shuffling. I can feel them listening. Miss Priss smiles stickily and smacks her lips.

'She says you're trying to earn enough money to go to New York City to audition for the ballet.'

I keep my mouth locked tight, but I bet the whole class can hear my heart thumping a beat against my skinny ribs, thump, thump, thump, trying to pound its way out of the room.

Miss Priss looks at her fingernails and says oh-so-casual like, 'My father just bought me a new audition outfit and shoes for New York. So we thought you could use some of my old ballet clothes, since they're so expensive.'

She drops the paper bag on the desk in front of me. There is steel in her voice.

'I think everything should fit,' she says, 'except the shoes. I don't know if they'll fit over your fat feet.'

'I don't need your help,' I say through tight teeth and push the bag away. Everyone is watching now. They aren't even pretending not to stare.

'Don't be silly, Casey,' Miss Priss says, all light and airy. 'I know how hard it is for your family. You don't have a father to support you like I do. So you can't afford to be so proud.' She turns with a swoosh of skirt. 'And if you have any manners at all, you'll remember to write a Thank You card,' she says over her shoulder. 'You can send it through my mother. That will save you the cost of a stamp.'

And at that, the worm does what it's wanted to do all day. It explodes.

I leap over my desk, not like a ballerina, but like a tiger. And it seems that before my feet even touch the floor, I am on top of her.

'I hate you,' I say as I push Miss Priss Ann-Lee with all the force of my leap, trying to dig my fingernails into her scrawny bird-neck.

She goes down, shrieking. She's not so snarky now. I try to jump on top of her to crush her into the ground. 'Get off me, you stupid hayseed,' she screams, and kicks me hard.

Her legs are strong, and I fly back against a desk. The rest of the class, shocked by the fight, come to life and gather around us, creating a wrestling ring in the middle of the class. I don't care. I hardly hear them. All I hear is the snarl in my throat as Miss Priss and I growl at each other, eyes blazing. How dare she? How dare she say we're poor? How dare she think I need her help? I don't need help from nobody.

'You're nothing but a no-good piece of trailer trash. I bet your mother wasn't even married to your father,' she hisses.

'My father died in the war,' I say. 'Where was your father?'

Ann-Lee's face goes white.

'He didn't even fight, did he?' I say, clawing at my hold on her. The class stares at her waiting for an answer.

'My father has diabetes. They wouldn't let him fight.'

I snort.

'He wanted to go,' Miss Priss says.

She shoves me, and I shove her back.

'Yeah, right. I bet he was *real* sad when he got to stay safe in South Carolina.'

The class is on my side now. I can feel them.

'I bet he was real sad when everyone else went to fight, and he got to stay here getting rich.'

'He did, he wanted to fight,' Ann-Lee screams, and launches herself at me. She's clawing and kicking. 'You don't know anything. You're just a stupid hayseed. You'll always be a hayseed. You'll never be a dancer.'

Miss Priss scratches her fingers on my neck. I hit back hard. I don't care about her father. I just want to hurt her. I want to make her sorry she said I was a hayseed. I want to hit her so hard that she'll fly away and never come back. I claw my way toward Ann-Lee's face.

I manage to get my fingers around that fancy ballet bun, and I pull hard until the band snaps and the hair falls loose. I wrap my hand around her hair real good. I am about to pull again, when another force drags me back. I lash out and realize, too late, that I've just punched Mr Richmond.

I watch as his glasses skitter to the floor in slow motion, a large crack running down the left lens. The room goes silent. Mr Richmond touches his eye where I've hit him, and I go limp. There's nothing else for me to do. Miss Priss starts crying and is taken to the nurse. I'm not crying, so I am taken to the principal's office.

As I wait outside, I feel something warm and wet slide down my face. For a moment, I think it is a tear. When I reach up and touch it, I am relieved. I am not crying. It is a bloody nose. I am no sissy crybaby like Miss Priss. I'm the winner.

The door opens, and I walk in to face Principal Haydon. He hands me a tissue.

'Fighting in school is very serious, Casey,' he says.

I nod. There is nothing I can say. *She gave me her old ballet clothes* is not an excuse for a fight. He wouldn't understand that it was the way she did it. Like I needed her help. I don't need help from no stuck-up Miss Priss who thinks she can dance just because she has new shoes.

'You're going to have to stay after school for detention,' he says.

Now I start to panic. 'I can't,' I say. 'I just got a job after school.' I keep talking before he can interrupt. 'I'll come in early,' I say, 'before school.'

He looks at me for a moment. He is thinking that my family is poor and I have to help. Normally, I would be angry about this. Mama and Gran take good care of me. We do just fine. But today I don't care. I need that job to go to the audition.

Finally, he says, 'Alright, Casey. Come in twenty minutes early, for a week. And be on time, or else it will be after school.'

I sigh with relief whooshing up to my ears.

'You'll stay in at recesses, too,' he says, just to prove he's still in charge.

But recess doesn't matter to me, not one bit. I can keep my job. My heart floats up with relief and I look down at my toes to hide my smile. I don't want Principal Haydon to think he's being too soft on me.

When I leave the office, I am surprised to see Miss Priss waiting her turn to see the principal. She is in trouble, too. Her hair is all snarled and stringy, and her eyes are red from crying like a crocodile. She looks at me quickly. Then she turns her head away, sniffing hard. Like she's trying not to cry. I turn on my heel and walk back to the classroom. She doesn't even deserve a second glance.

Back in the classroom, I am alone. The air is hot and sticky, and the shades are drawn against the afternoon sun. Three flies buzz hopelessly against the glass. Bashing themselves to pieces trying to get free. I know how they feel. The brown paper bag is still on my desk. Since I am alone, I look inside.

Folded neatly at the bottom is a small pile of pink.

Tights, leotard, a floaty skirt, and a pair of pink satin slippers. It is all so perfect. I want to reach out and touch the fabric, to try on the shoes, to spin around the classroom with beauty and grace and never stop until I'm dancing in New York City. Then I look again and see the nametag sewn into the back of the leotard: *Ann-Lee Ryder*. The words feel like a punch in the gut. I will not wear her old clothes. It'd be like putting on a snake's old skin.

I carry the bag to the window and shoo the flies into the air outside. I watch them fly away in giant loops. Then I lean out the window and tip the bag over. I watch Miss Priss's ballet clothes fall into the open dumpster below, landing softly on top of the mound of trash. I don't need her to get to New York City. I don't need anyone or anything except myself, my dreams and my two feet.

Chapter Six

It is not Mama who makes me go back to the dumpster. It is Gran.

I tell her about the fight at school because I think she will understand. But when I tell her about tipping the ballet clothes into the dumpster, she stops me.

'I am ashamed of you, Casey,' she says.

I expected Gran to laugh until her arms wobbled, to hug me and be proud. I stood up for myself. I stood up for our family.

'She treated me like a beggar,' I say. 'In front of the whole class.'

'And you're going to let a little thing like that get in the way of your dreams?'

We are sitting in the janitor's office on Gran's

ten-minute break. Everything smells of coffee and bleach.

'Casey, you have a dream, and you have a chance to make it come true. A real good chance. Not everyone gets that. So don't tell me you're gonna throw that chance away just to spite Ann-Lee.'

It smarts when Gran says that. I hate thinking Gran is disappointed in me. That's lower than anything. But I still don't understand why she wants me to take charity from Miss Priss Ann-Lee. Mama says we don't need to take nobody's charity, that we get along just fine. Mama's real proud because she's real strong. She takes care of all of us.

After my father died the church ladies tried to bring us food for Thanksgiving, but Mama would have none of that. She said there were plenty of people worse off than us, and that as long as she was alive her family wouldn't go hungry. Besides, she said, they never offered any help while he was away fighting, so why should we take their help now that he was dead? Mama hated their smiles like they were doing us some big favor, like they were going to go home and give each other big smug pats on the back. Mama stopped going to church after that. And after a while the church ladies stopped dropping by to see if we needed help. It's a long walk to our house from the middle of town. But Mama always says it doesn't matter, that we have each other and we don't need help from anyone else. I want to be strong like Mama. I want to get to New York City on my own. I clench my fists hard against my sides.

'Casey,' says Gran, 'I know you don't want to take help from Ann-Lee, but what if you can't get ballet clothes? What then? Will you forget about the audition? That would be like letting Ann-Lee take your dream away herself.'

'But if she sees me wearing her clothes at the audition . . .' I try to explain.

Gran cuts in. 'What? Why are you so worried about what Ann-Lee thinks, Casey?'

'She called me a hayseed and trailer trash.' The words are so hateful, my voice wobbles as I say them.

'Well,' says Gran. 'Are you?'

'No,' I say. I can feel the bad feelings shrivel up inside me, and somehow I feel very small without them. Gran puts her arms around my shoulders, and I let out a big sigh.

'Then don't worry what Ann-Lee thinks,' Gran says. 'She's got her own problems to worry about.'

I laugh. Ann-Lee has a mother and a father and money for lessons. What does she have to worry about? But Gran just shakes her head. She shakes it like she feels sorry for Miss Priss. Then she sighs.

'You need to decide what's more important, Casey. Your pride. Or your dreams. That's all. Once you decide that, the rest will be easy.' Gran smiles. 'Now you get to work. Mr Crampton won't take kindly to too much chit-chat in the office.'

I start to go, then I remember Miss Priss's mother. 'Gran, what about Mrs Ryder? Won't she be mad about the fight?'

'She's been here since eight this morning, so Ann-Lee can't have blabbed to her yet. You're safe, honey-bear, for today anyhow.'

I know Gran is always right, but I still give a start when Mrs Ryder's voice says hello from the nurses' station.

'Hello,' I say, quiet and cautious. Miss Priss could have run here straight from school just to get me in trouble.

'I thought you'd like to know that Mr Homes isn't in his room today.' Her eyes twinkle at me, and crinkle up into a smile. 'So you can practice your dancing all you want.'

I smile back. I feel a little guilty. Not about beating up Miss Priss – she had that coming to her, in spades! But it seems wrong to be having such a nice talk with her mother and not telling her what happened. I bet she wouldn't be so nice if she knew. It doesn't really matter, though. Miss Priss will tell her soon enough. I bet she's sitting at home just waiting to snitch on me. I don't understand why Gran feels sorry for Miss Priss at all. She's a no good rat-fink. And that's that.

I say thank you to Mrs Ryder and disappear up the hall. I grit my teeth hard, and then I get to work.

I start sweeping the rooms, working my way up from the very end of the hall. At first I just go hard and fast, scrubbing angry. But soon I'm back to my broom dance, sweeping each room in time to the beeping machines. Today some of the people in the rooms are awake.

At first, I am careful. I don't want to annoy anyone like I did with Mr Homes. But I can't help moving to the beat. None of these patients seems to mind, though. Some of them even cheer me on. I forget about Miss Priss and our fight. I even forget how angry I am. All I feel is the rhythm in my toe bones, tapping up through my spine.

When I am done with all the rooms, I feel like I've just given a performance on a royal stage. I curtsey low and imagine applause filling the air. And there is applause. The woman in the bed is clapping for me.

'You've brightened up my whole day, dearie,' she says.

I smile, bow again, and sweep out of the room. I call back over my shoulder as I go, 'Encore performance, same time tomorrow.'

Is it worth giving this up just so Miss Priss doesn't

make fun of me? It seems like a silly question now. I stop at the white desk where Mrs Ryder is filling out forms. 'Mrs Ryder,' I say. 'I forgot to thank you for giving me Ann-Lee's old ballet things.'

She smiles at me, and this time I don't feel so guilty. As I leave, I wonder how such a nice woman ended up with such an annoying daughter. A stinkbug must've crawled into Miss Priss's crib when she was a baby.

I walk back to the school without even realizing it. My feet point me to the dumpster and I follow them. Step. Step. Step. Left. Right. Left. Gran. Is. Right.

The playground is empty now; all the other kids have gone home. I scramble into the dumpster without even thinking about it. My dream is what's important. And I'll make it come true any way I can.

When I crunch into the dumpster, I discover that other people have thrown things away. The pink ballet tights and leotard are smeared with Miracle Whip, and something greasy has slid into one of the shoes. The Sloppy Joes no one finished at lunch squelch around my toes, and the smell makes me gag. I am tempted to leave the clothes there. Even when they were clean they were like Miss Priss's discarded snakeskin, and now they are just gross, but I remember what Gran said and carry them home holding my nose.

When I get home, Gran is cooking dinner because Mama is working the night shift this week. The kitchen is full of the sound of Perry Como crooning on the radio. Gran doesn't say anything when I come in with the smelly pink mess, but I see her smile. I know she's proud of me. I put the ballet clothes and everything I'm wearing right in the washtub, then scrub my hands until they're pink. I put on clean clothes and go back to the kitchen to help Gran with dinner.

She is making macaroni with extra cheese and real butter, not the vegetable oil Mama uses. There's sweet potato mash with sour cream to go on the side and a mountain of sweet baby peas. And since Gran is cooking, I know there'll be dessert.

I set two places at the table. Dancing with the plates as I lay them out. Then I go sit on the counter to watch Gran's great arms wobble as she mashes the potatoes, swaying in time to the music. Mr C's voice, rich as gravy, sings 'Catch a Falling Star'.

'Here, Casey.' She hands me the pot. 'You mash for a bit. Your gran needs a rest.' She sits down huffing and puffing while I finish the potatoes.

'Don't be stingy with the sour cream,' she says. And I'm not.

'Mama's not gonna be happy,' I say.

'You leave your mama to me,' says Gran.

'I mean about me being in trouble at school.'

'So do I.' Gran winks at me.

We eat as soon as I finish the potatoes. I don't say anything when Gran has seconds, and she doesn't say anything about my toes dancing under the table. They slide side to side. Everything is too delicious to keep them still. I go to bed too full to think about what to tell Mama when I have to leave early for detention in the morning.

I wake up when Mama comes home after the night shift.

I can hear her cooking me breakfast before she goes to bed. I shuffle-step down the stairs, trying to keep my steps light and happy. But I always dance how I feel. And I feel guilty. Mama's gonna be mad when she finds out I got detention.

I eat breakfast without a word. I can tell Mama is tired because she doesn't even look to see why I'm being so quiet and sitting so still. Two sure signs that I am up to something.

I am about to blurt everything out when Gran comes in.

'What are you doing up so early?' Mama asks her.

'Casey said she'd get up early and take a walk with me before she goes to school.'

- 56 -

'Well, it'll do you good after the dinner you ate last night. You know what the doctor said about cheese. And all that butter. It isn't good for you.'

'Don't nag, Caroline,' Gran says as she shoos me out the door.

This is how it is.

Every morning Gran and I go straight to school. I go to detention while Gran sits at Willy's General Store counter drinking cups of coffee with cream and making small talk with the other customers. It seems like everyone knows Gran. Every afternoon I go to the hospital, clean the recovery ward and dance for the patients. I stop feeling so guilty, too. Now that I'm sharing my secret with Gran, it feels like less of a lie.

Mrs Ryder never gets mad at me about the fight, and I learn that Miss Priss didn't tell her about it because she got in trouble, too. She couldn't nark on me without narking on herself. So everything is fine. Or at least, everything is fine until Thursday, two days before the audition.

I am cleaning the hospital and giving the patients a beautiful recital. I forget to check that Mr Homes is gone before I go inside. I burst into his room with a flying leap. It is payday and I am on my way to New York City. No more sweeping smelly hospital floors. No more nothing-ever-happens Warren.

Mr Homes is sitting in his bed, buttoned up in his striped pajamas. He smiles as he presses the blue button that calls the nurse.

Mrs Ryder isn't here today, and another nurse comes in. She is a sour woman with steel-grey hair and a mouth like all she eats is lemon. She's big, too, but not big like Gran. Gran is happy and wears her weight well; this woman just lumbers in like a bear. The buttons on her white nurse's uniform look like they might pop off. She looks at Mr Holmes and asks him what he wants.

'I would like to speak to the man in charge of cleaning,' he says, still smiling. I growl inside my head. He is having fun getting me in trouble.

The nurse just grunts and walks away.

I bite my tongue, but I can't keep quiet. 'How old are you?' I ask.

'Excuse me?' He squints his bug eyes at me.

'I said, how old are you?' I am tapping my right foot. My arms are crossed. I am MAD. Who does he think he is?

'That's none of your business.' Mr Homes crosses his arms right back at me, all acid and vinegar.

'Fine,' I say. 'You look about seventy.'

'I'm fifty-six!' I can see I got him there. His face goes tomato-red, a real prize-winner, too.

'Well, bad temper makes you age.'

'Do you have a point?' He's red enough to take the blue ribbon now.

'Yes. You are too old to have such bad manners. You enjoy making other people unhappy. And that is just sad.' I turn on my heel and skip out the door. What do I care what cranky Mr Homes says? They can fire me today if they want to. The hospital still has to pay me for all my work. That's the law.

I smile and carry the broom in a victory dance all the way back to the janitor's office. But when I open the door, my insides fall down into my shoes. Mr Crampton is waiting for me, and he doesn't look happy.

Chapter Seven

Slap. Stamp. Splash. My feet hit the earth in time to my tears, kicking the red dust along the side of the road.

Mr Crampton did not fire me. He docked my pay. I am fifty cents short of a bus ticket, and New York City is drifting away. I kick out hard, trying to stab my heels into the dirt. It isn't fair. I even offered to apologize to Mr Homes, but Mr Crampton wouldn't listen. I roar inside, thinking how on earth could that measly man be the one to tie my toes here in no-good, nothing-ever-happens, no-one-ever-changes Warren.

When I burst through the door, both Mama and Gran look at me. I am a shuddering mess. My eyes feel red-raw and my nose is running. When I see their faces, my knees collapse. But I don't hit the floor. Mama's by my side in an instant.

She catches me up in her arms. And when Mama gets her arms around me I start crying, because it's too much to hold onto by myself.

'Casey, what's wrong?'

I blubber, too upset to care about tears or my runny nose. I tell them about Mr Homes and Mr Crampton, and how I'm not going to New York City after all. Even after fishing Miss Priss's stinky snakeskin ballet clothes out of the dumpster. Even after cleaning the recovery ward every day. When I am finished explaining, I take a deep breath and let Mama rock me back and forth. I am too worn down to rock myself.

Gran is very quiet. She looks at me, then she makes a noise, *harrumphing* like a settling hippo. She pulls her shawl off the hook where she hangs it every night when she comes home from work.

'Right,' she says, wrapping that shawl around her shoulders like a bullfighter going into battle. 'Casey, you eat something and get to bed. You've got a big day tomorrow. I'll be back.' Then she walks out the door, letting the screen slam behind her.

I look at Mama, but Mama is quiet as a raindrop. She sits me down at the table and puts a bowl of soup in front of me.

'Eat,' she says, turning back to the ironing.

I am not hungry, but I fill the spoon and put it in my

mouth. The warm broth slides past the lump in my throat, and I fill the spoon again. All I can think about is having to go back and beg Mrs Ryder for a ride, and she'll probably say no. Miss Priss will tell her about the fight. I can feel the tears starting to leak down my face. I sniff hard and push away the rest of the soup. Mama leads me to my room.

I feel light as I float along the hall, but not with joy. I am empty, less than empty. I am a bubble that has just burst but still remembers its shape.

On the chair in my room, Gran has laid out Ann-Lee's ballet clothes, but they aren't Ann-Lee's anymore. Gran has given the leotard a deep V in the front and the back. She has taken the floaty, wraparound skirt and sewn it around the leotard, gathering it together in the back. It looks like something an Egyptian princess would wear. Only the shoes still look like they belonged to someone else, and now that I know I can't wear them, this stings even more.

I put on my jim-jams and climb into bed. Mama sits on the sheets next to me. It is strange to have her there beside me. Her eyes are thoughtful and sad as she looks at the painted trees. It's like she is staring through them, at something else, something very far away. Then she sighs and looks at me.

'I'm sorry, Casey,' she says, smoothing the sheet at my

side. 'But maybe this is for the best.'

I am too sad and too tired to argue, but how can it be for the best? Everything is in New York City. New York City is the stars.

'Sometimes, Casey, people spend their whole lives living for a dream they can't have. And these people are so busy, so greedy for their dream that they forget all the good things they already have.'

'But . . .' I start to argue. I can't see what's wrong with dreaming.

Mama just sighs. 'Get some sleep, Casey. You're all worn out.'

She gets up and clicks off the light, leaving me in the dark. I wonder if Mama ever had a dream, or if she always thought like she thinks now, that dreams are dangerous and a bad idea.

I am still awake when Gran comes home. I hear the screen door creak open. Mama's feet pad down the hall past my door. If I sit up and take my head off the pillow, I can hear them talking in the kitchen.

'I got the money.' Gran's voice is rich as gravy, and I cling to my knees with hope.

'How?' I can see Mama in my head. Her arms are folded tight across her chest. One foot is tapping on the floor. She's mad at Gran, but she can't say so. Not straight out, at least.

'Never mind how,' Gran says. 'I got the money, and now Casey can go to that audition.'

In the silence my heart overflows into my lungs and I have to hold the pillow over my face to keep quiet. I *can* go. My whole body wants to wriggle about. It wants to dance. Right now. But I keep still. Mama and Gran aren't done talking yet.

Mama says, 'You shouldn't build her up like this. How is she supposed to get through that audition? And even if she does, you know we can't afford for her to live in New York.'

'Do you want her spending the rest of her life in this town, mopping that hospital floor till she's worn out as a rag herself?'

I can hear Gran sit down heavy in one of the kitchen chairs. Mama doesn't move. She doesn't make a sound, and Gran keeps talking.

'Casey's going places. One way or another. She's got something real big inside her, and I'm going to make sure it gets out. You should be making sure, too.'

Mama interrupts Gran before she's done with her last word. It's the first time I've ever heard Mama yelling at Gran. 'She's not a little girl anymore. She's old enough to know what the real world is like. At some point we all have to give up our dreams.'

'Don't be ridiculous,' Gran yells right back at Mama, real ferocious. My heart is pounding hard enough to escape.

'Ridiculous?' Mama stops. I can hear her take a breath in the silent house. Then her voice goes low. 'You know what I had to give up for this family.'

'You didn't have to give up anything, Caroline. You chose to and you know it.'

'What was I supposed to do, Mama? What was I supposed to do when Richard died? I had to get a real job to support us all.' My skin goes cold. Mama never talks about my father.

'That was ten years ago,' Gran says. 'How many times has Mr Crampton asked you to paint up the children's ward since then? How many times have you said no?'

'That's not the point,' Mama says. Her voice is tired.

'That is exactly the point. You gave up on dreaming the day Richard died. I understand that. But you have a daughter, Caroline. It's time for you to start dreaming again. Even if it's only for her. Casey is going to that audition, and that's final.' Gran slams something down on the kitchen table. I can hear it echo through the house like a shot.

Mama is quiet.

'Go to bed, Caroline.' Gran says it like she is shaking her head. Like she's disappointed in Mama. I wonder if Gran thought Mama had something big inside her, too.

Something bigger than cleaning hospital floors in boring old Warren.

Footsteps sound up the hallway to my room. I slam myself back down, pretending to be asleep. The door opens, and I can tell by the heavy steps that it's Gran.

'Casey, I know you're not sleeping.' Gran sits down, and my mattress groans. She holds up two round quarters.

'How did you get it?' I ask, as Gran puts the money in my hand.

'I explained very nicely to Mr Homes how much going to New York City meant to you, and he wanted to make up for getting you in trouble.'

Even in the dark, I can see her eyes twinkle. I doubt very much that what she said to Mr Homes was nice at all. 'Did he really just give you the money, Gran?' I ask.

Gran grunts and fusses with the covers, tucking them tight up to my chin. 'Well, I wouldn't say he just gave it to me. He is the sourest man I have ever met. Accused me of being a Communist. Can you imagine?'

I laugh.

'I had to give him a piece of my mind after that, and in the end he saw reason,' says Gran with a big grin. 'Now you get some sleep.'

Gran levers herself off the bed. As she opens the door, light from the hallway spills in around her edges, lighting her up like an angel.

'Gran,' I say, and she turns. 'Thank you for the ballet clothes. They're almost like new the way you fixed them.'

'Almost?' Gran puts her hands on her hips, pretending to be cross.

'Well,' I say. 'I still wish I could have gotten new ballet slippers. You know. My own pair.'

'Casey, if it bugs you that much, why don't you just audition in your old high-tops. You're always dancing in them anyway.'

'Gran! You can't do *ballet* in high-tops.'

'Well then, Ann-Lee's slippers will have to do.' Gran smiles with her voice.

I roll my eyes, but I know Gran is right. Going to the audition is way more important than feeling bad about wearing Miss Priss's hand-me-down shoes. I might not like wearing them, but I won't let that stop me dancing. And once I'm a prima ballerina I can buy all the new ballet slippers I want.

'Gran,' I say softly. 'What dream did Mama give up?'

Gran looks through the dark room into the distant mountains painted on my wall. 'Not tonight, Casey. We'll talk about it when you come back from New York City.'

But from the way she stares at my mama's painting, I think I already know.

Chapter Eight

I wake up early, before the sun peeks into my bedroom. When I sit up, I'm jangling all over. Today I am getting on a bus to audition for The School of American Ballet. I shiver out of bed and get dressed in the dark. I can feel my new ballet clothes waiting for me. I am so excited I hardly remember someone else has worn them.

Without turning on the light, I hold onto the foot of my bed and start to stretch. First my arms and my back. Then my legs. I kick each one high into the air, and as I do I see the first line of the sun appear in my window. It is so bright and beautiful it makes the painted water on my wall sparkle. I kick even harder to hurry the sun along. Wake up, lazybones. Today is a day for shining!

Everything goes fast once the sun is up. I am into my

best traveling dress, blue-and-white striped with a blue belt. Gran let the hem out for me again, so my knobbly knees are covered. I can't hardly eat a bite of breakfast, my stomach is dancing so. But I make myself swallow, for strength. I have to ride all night to get to New York City by tomorrow.

School crawls by like a lazy fly in the sun. Miss Priss isn't here. Mrs Ryder took her out of school today so they could get to New York City early. So Miss Priss could be fresh for the audition. All the freshness in the world won't stop her feet from flopping. Mrs Ryder asked if I wanted to ride with them, but I wouldn't be caught dead in a car with Miss Priss sitting in the front, telling me not to touch anything and gloating over how I'd have never gotten to the audition without her. And I don't even want to think about sharing a hotel room with Miss Priss. I'll take the bus, thank you very much.

I look at the clock every chance I get. It hardly seems to move at all until, suddenly, it is three o'clock and the bell rings. Mama and Gran are waiting for me outside the schoolyard and we walk together to Willy's General Store to wait for the bus.

We don't say much while we walk. My mouth is dry as a desert. I don't think I could say a word if I wanted to.

Mama had been quiet all morning, too. She didn't

hardly say a word at breakfast, and now she is silent as can be. I haven't had time to think about it, but now that we are stuck waiting for the bus, I wonder if she's mad at me. I twist and turn nervously. The window of Willy's General Store is full of the new products for summer. A fishing pole and a picnic basket sit on top of a pile of canning jars for summer jam. In one dusty corner, I see a set of paints and brushes. I stare hard at the paints. Someday I'm gonna come back to Warren, after I'm a famous ballerina. I'm gonna come back and buy Mama that paint set.

The bus comes wheezing around the corner in a cloud of road dust. Heatwaves shimmer off its side. Mama leans forward. 'Here's your dinner and your lunch, and some extra snacks in case you get hungry.' She hands me a brown paper sack, heavy with sandwiches. 'And this is for something extra.' She puts two shiny dimes in the palm of my hand. They click together as I close my fist. I look at Mama, my eyes wide. She must have been saving that for something special, and then I smile because Mama gave it to me.

Mama straightens up. 'Now don't go and fritter that all away on snacks. You find something really special. Something you'll remember forever.'

I nod.

Gran wraps me up in her arms and squeezes me hard. 'Good luck, Casey,' she says, and I smile.

She squeezes me one more time, so hard I can hardly breathe, and then she lets me go. 'Now you go show New York what you're made of.'

She squeezes me again, and then Mama does, too. I don't think they'll ever stop until the bus horn blasts so loud we all jump. I hurry up and climb aboard, clutching my ticket tight in the hot palm of my hand as I walk to the back of the bus.

I press my nose against the glass and wave until Mama and Gran are two dots in the distance. I even watch after they are gone. I am on the bus to New York City, and my toes go tippity-tap. The man next to me gives me the look to sit still, but I don't care. I am on my way over the moon, and no grumped-up man and his briefcase are gonna bring me down. I tap my toes as much as I please, and wonder what I'll find that's special enough to buy with Mama's twenty cents.

It's hot on the bus. Even the breeze coming in through the windows feels sluggish and wet. The seat is hard, and pretty soon I can feel my legs and my back going stiff. I want to stand up and stretch, but the man next to me scowls when I so much as twitch a toe, so instead I take a good look at the other people on the bus.

A few seats in front of me is a woman holding a crying baby. She's got a big suitcase on the metal rack above her head, and I wonder where she is going. She looks tired but hopeful, and I think she must be, like me, on the start of a big adventure.

There are other people on the bus who don't look excited at all, like they do this every day. Men in suits and hats going up to the big city to do big business. Families going to visit relatives two towns over. My eyes dart from person to person, trying to guess their stories.

Outside the world flies by, budding fields of cotton and corn. The bus's wheels hum against the road. Every few towns, we pull over into one dusty parking lot or another, and some people get off and others get on. I watch through the window and everyone is hugging, saying hello or goodbye. I wonder what we looked like, Mama, Gran and me. Probably just like any normal family. I bet no one knew they were looking at Casey Quinn, New York City's next prima ballerina. But they were.

And then I wonder who I'm looking at. All these people must have their dreams, too. And maybe that's why they are on the bus to New York City. Maybe they want to be dancers, or singers, or run big companies, or sell inventions. It's strange to try to think of everyone else like that, like my brain isn't big enough to hold all their stories together inside my head, and it makes me feel a bit wobbly to try and imagine all the hopes and dreams that fill up this bus. I close my eyes and float back into my own head.

It's really happening.

My whole body leaps with excitement. I am sitting on a bus to New York City on my way to audition for The School of American Ballet. My toes tap against the floor, and I sit on my hands to keep them still. As the sun sinks lower and lower, the bus stops less and less. Soon all I can see are the lights of passing cars, rushing by my window in a gentle rhythm. I feel my head drifting back and forth, and I let it rest against the window, feeling the hum of the bus against my temples, slowly soothing me to sleep.

I wake up the next morning, and my toes are still tapping. The bus stops hard, and the suitcases in the metal rack above my head shift and slide into each other. I hug my knapsack to my chest, as people yawn and stretch around me. The driver calls out, 'Port Authority!' The bus is filled with the sound of people waking up, and the stale, sour smell of sitting still for too long.

I stand up careful as can be, testing my legs. I am worried they will be stiff and slow. But they are springier than ever. I want to leap down the aisle, but there isn't space. Instead I take my bag, and file off the bus like everyone else.

In the station there is a large round desk with a sign that reads 'Information'. I ask a woman with long pink nails directions to the ballet studio, which isn't too far from here. She smiles and points me toward a large metal door so big I bet you could have driven the bus straight through it. I straighten my knapsack and my shoulders, and walk out the door. And I am in the City!

Chapter Nine

For a moment I can't even move. It is bigger than I ever imagined it. There are people everywhere, their heels going *clickity-clackity*, mumbling as they rush past me. Important places to go! Important people to see! A blue sedan swoops past, blowing up a wind around my ankles, carrying a crumpled-up newspaper page down the street. The wind seems to push me forward. *Keep up. You're in New York City*, it says. *Get moving!*

At first I walk up the sidewalk slowly, trying to see everything. Usually my feet are flying, running through Warren, 'cause it's too boring to bother looking at. But not New York. The buildings stretch themselves to the clouds, and I tip my head back to look at them. Signs full of electric lights flashing ads for Coca-Cola and Shulton

Old Spice shaving cream are up there, reaching out for the whole city to see. I bet you can see those signs for miles.

I walk with my eyes fixed on the sky, bumping my way along. People push past me, all unfriendly. They're rushing down the streets of the City like it's any other town in America. My mouth is wide open, but I don't care. How can everyone just rush along and not look at things? Don't they know where they are?

I feel smaller than small looking up at the sky. Warren is just a blip compared to New York City. Even the air seems bigger here. It is so full of sounds and smells. A man stands on the corner with a big metal box on wheels selling hot dogs; a boy has a chair set up on the corner and is shining shoes. The rattle-clatter of steps, *extra extra, shine your shoes, hot dogs, get your fresh hot dogs.* Everyone is yelling and shouting at the crowd racing past.

And the air is full of something else, too. A buzz, an energy. And once I feel it, my feet start moving faster. Catching onto the groove of New York City until I'm a part of the hustle and bustle, too. I'm racing along, moving to the faster beat of the city, feet hardly skimming the sidewalk.

When I get to the corner, I can see people pouring up onto the sidewalk from a set of secret steps that disappear underground. And another lot pouring down into the darkness. It makes me shiver. The crowd behind me surges forward, pushing me toward the hot, smelly steps. I try to side-step away. I want to stay in the sun, not go down some stinky hole, but the crowd is too strong and I get carried forward like I'm nothing but a leaf on a river.

I fight back panic. I don't want to go down underground, but the crowd doesn't seem to notice I'm there. Everyone is pushing and shoving, and my feet go forward by themselves. The steps are slick with steam and worn shiny by people's feet.

I stumble down the steps, eyes blinking in the darkness. The air is roaring as a silver bullet squeals into the station. The crowd pushes me forward through a revolving metal gate. Doors open, and people pour on and off of the train. I tell my feet to stay still, and lean back into the crowd, refusing to move no matter where they push me. But it's no use. I am swept onto the train. The doors shut, and the floor lurches beneath me.

Outside the window, I can see the platform sweep away, and then only darkness. The train snakes away beneath my feet, shooting under the city. My heart pounds inside my chest, and I'm sure someone must realize I'm not supposed to be here, but when I look around, no one looks back. They have their faces stuck into big grey newspapers, and don't seem to mind at all when the train jerks beneath their feet. It's all I can do to stay standing up.

I move to the door, squeezing through the crowd and pressing myself against the glass. No one is going to help me here, I think, and I square my shoulders like a soldier. I bend my knees to absorb the bumps, and get ready for the train to stop.

The train roars along, chugging and chattering, screeching and squawking. I don't know how anyone can read with this racket. We seem to go on for ages, and I wonder if the train will ever stop. The car sways sharp to the left, and I bump into a woman knitting a bright green scarf. She doesn't even look up.

Finally, the next station flashes into sight and the train jerks to a halt. I tumble against the door, but stay on my feet, and when the doors open I am free. No polite *after you* for me. I am off the train and pushing my way to the front of the crowd.

I press myself against the wall as people push past. This time my feet listen when I tell them to keep still, and I wait for the crowd to die down. There is a roaring behind me, and the train is gone. The last of the people disappear up the steps and my heart pounds loud in the empty cavern under the city. The subway smells like moldy bread and old wash-water. I look around.

I can see a small square of blue at the top of the stairway, and I make my way toward it on shaky legs. Blinking hard when I come up into the sun. All around me I can see green, trees and grass, and a large golden statue that shimmers in the early morning sun. I can hear the breeze rustling the leaves just like back home, and birds chirping from high above me. My heart leaps up into my mouth. How far has the train taken me? This doesn't look like New York City at all. Tears sting my eyes.

I run forward, feet flying over the ground, looking for a way back to the city. A flock of grey birds scatter as I run through them. They spiral up above me, and then land again once I am gone. I could get back on the train, but that might take me even further away, and I shudder, imagining going back down those steps.

People walk past me, but slow and calm, not like the people in the city at all. Women push big black strollers under the trees, and older boys and girls wander hand in hand.

I wander forward, further into the green, until I find a bench, and then I sit down. I feel very small and very lost, and I wonder how will I ever get back to New York City, and if I can't get back there, how will I ever get home to Mama and Gran. I miss them, sudden and fierce and a teardrop splashes against the back of my hand.

'You all right, kid?' someone asks from above me.

I look up and see a boy. He's fifteen or sixteen, just a few years older than me and just as freckled. He's sitting on some sort of a cart hitched up to a beautiful bay mare. The cart is sleek and black with soft red seats on the inside, and large silver bells running along the harness. And now I know for sure I'm not in the City. Who ever heard of a horse in New York? The tears bubble up again, and I bite my lip hard to keep them down. I will not cry, no matter what.

The boy jumps down from the cart and walks over to me. Mama warned me not to talk to strangers in the City. It's a mean place, she said. But the boy doesn't look mean, and I'm not in the City anyway.

'What's the problem?' he asks, scratching the mare with one lazy hand.

I take a deep breath and look at his face. He doesn't look like he's up to no good, or a dressed-up devil trying to steal my soul. His clothes look worn and patched but clean, and shaded by a grey wool cap. I hold that breath in and my toes start tapping. I don't really have a choice. I need to tell someone, and maybe this boy can help. I let my breath out and the words come tumbling with it.

'I came to New York City to audition for the ballet

school, but I got caught in a crowd and pushed underground and,' I fight hard to keep my voice strong, 'and when I got off the train, I was here.' I look around at all of the plants. 'And I don't know how to get back.'

The boy's freckled face cracks open into a smile, and then he starts to laugh. A great rolling sound that gathers speed like a wave. My face goes hot to the tips of my ears, and I'm not scared anymore. I'm mad. I stand up.

I walk away fast and then start to run, moving uphill further into the trees. I'll find my own way back to the City. Even if it means getting back on that train. I can hear him crashing after me, but I don't care. I will not stand still and listen to someone laughing at me, not for all the corn in Kansas. My face is red from running now, but I don't stop. I'm heading back to the stairway underground. Back to my audition and back to New York City.

Chapter Ten

'Wait,' the boy calls after me, but I don't listen. I didn't work for weeks in that smelly old hospital and come miles and miles on a bus to be laughed at. My feet tear at the ground like mad dogs, but the thorns and branches keep slowing me down. The stairs aren't where I remember, and now I feel more lost than before.

I need to stop and think, but he's still following me. I wish that Mama and Gran were here. I wouldn't even mind seeing Miss Priss, I think for a moment, and then I step down hard on that. If I never saw Miss Priss's cow eyes again it would be too soon.

'Wait,' he calls again, closer this time.

I turn on the heel of my foot, so fast the world spins.

'What?' I say, hands on hips, feet forward in fighting stance.

'I'm sorry I laughed,' he says. And his face does look sorry. 'But you see, you still *are* in New York City.'

I stare at the trees, and the green grass, and bright flowers that run along the side of the path. Then I look at the boy and roll my eyes. 'I may only be from Warren, South Carolina, but I'm no dope,' I say.

'No really, it is. This is Central Park,' he says. 'It's in the very middle of the City.'

I keep my face disbelieving, because I won't be teased. But I go all light with hope just the same.

'Come on,' he says. 'I'll show you.'

He grabs my hand and pulls me toward his carriage. Part angry, part relieved, and part something else all together. No one's ever held my hand before, not counting Mama and Gran. Especially not a boy.

He helps me up onto the front of his cart, and climbs up on the seat next to me, nudging the mare with a gentle click of his tongue.

'My name's Mike,' he says.

'I'm Casey,' I say softly. I know I shouldn't be going with him. But at least in a cart I can see where we're headed.

'Pleased to meet you, Casey,' Mike says.

The cart moves through the trees along the path quickly, and I struggle to take it all in. One moment we are riding quietly in the park, and the next moment we leave the trees and I see it. New York is there. Cars rush past us, coming oh-so-close, but the mare doesn't seem to mind at all, and now there is no roof over my head I can look up and see the tops of the buildings, higher than high in the sky.

We stop at the edge of the park, and I stare across the road to the other side where the buildings seem to block out the sun.

'Your first time in the City, huh?' Mike says.

I just nod. I don't have any words left.

'Where are you headed?'

'I'm going to The School of American Ballet,' I say, reciting the address I memorized from the audition notice. My fingers dancing the words as I say them, toes tapping 'cause I can't keep them still.

'Alright,' Mike says. 'It's not far from here, either. I can take you there for 25 cents.'

My heart skips a beat and my face goes blank.

'I don't have 25 cents,' I say. My voice feels small. Is everything in the city so expensive?

'Well, I might be able to do it for 20 . . .' He makes a face like he would be doing me a big favor. I can feel the two dimes Mama gave me tingling in my pocket, but I don't reach for them, not yet.

Mike scowls. Another horse and cart is clip-clopping toward us, driven by a man with greasy hair slicked back from one ear to the other.

'What are you doing here, Mikey?' the man says, his voice as greasy as his hair. 'This is my patch.'

'I've got a fare, Cooper,' Mike says. 'Picked her up back in the park, so don't try to pull anything fast.'

Mike goes to snap the reins, but I'm too quick for him.

'How much would you charge to take me to The School of American Ballet?' I ask the man.

The man smiles all slow and slithery. 'Well,' he says. Part of me wants him to say something low, because Mama would have my hide if she found out I spent my 20 cents on a ride to the audition. But the other part of me wants him to say something high, because I don't want to get in his carriage, not one bit. 'For a pretty thing like you, I could do it for ten cents . . .'

My heart sinks into my shoes. But before I can get out of the cart Mike is shouting, 'That's highway robbery, Cooper, and you know it! Anyway, she's my fare and that's that.'

Mike snaps the reins and the bay mare moves forward at a trot, leaving the greasy man in the dust behind us.

Mike glares straight forward like his eyes are glued to the road. I stare at him hard, trying to make him turn around with my eyes. He won't budge.

'You tried to charge me 25 cents,' I say, arms crossed.

Mike looks straight down the road like he didn't hear me at all, but I'm having none of that. I didn't come to the city to be laughed at, and I certainly didn't come here to be cheated. I eyeball him hard until he starts to squirm.

'Aw, don't be sore, Casey. I'm just trying to make a living.'

I keep glaring.

'Don't look at me like that,' he says. Then, 'Fine, I'll do it for ten.'

'You said ten was highway robbery,' I say. 'I'll give you a nickel. Take it or leave it.'

Mike is quiet for a moment, then he shakes his head and sighs. 'All right, you've got a deal.'

We both look back at the road, but I can feel him staring at me out of the corner of his eye. He's looking at my knobbly knees bouncing along to the horse's hooves clip-clopping on the hard sidewalk, and thinking, *This girl is no match for New York City Ballet*. His stare itches at my skin until I can't stand it anymore.

'What?' I ask, all sour and sharp.

Mike smiles slowly, like I am some sort of odd joke.

'You sure this is your first time to New York?' he asks.

'Of course I'm sure. Don't you think I'd know if I'd been here before?'

'Calm down there,' he says, raising his hands like he's protecting himself. His eyes twinkle at me. 'I'm just saying you fit right in.'

I am quiet. I think it must be the nicest thing anyone has ever said to me. I can feel a smile growing inside me, somewhere way down deep where it doesn't show. I am Casey Quinn. I am in New York City. And I belong.

Chapter Eleven

Mike whistles and the bay turns right, and left and right again, taking us down the wide street among the streams of cars. In front of us I can see a tall building, crystal-blue and shining in the afternoon sun. It rises up and up, high above the buildings around it, and at the top it gets narrower and narrower until it looks like a needle threading the clouds.

'That's the Empire State Building,' Mike says when he sees me staring. 'It's the tallest building in the world. You can pay to go to the top, you know.'

My insides wobble just thinking about being that far away from the ground, and I wonder if there is a railing to keep you from falling over the side.

The cart keeps moving and now I look closer to the

ground. We are going by shop after shop. Each one has a big glass window and a fancy display inside. And each display is miles bigger than Willy's General Store. I lean out of the carriage, looking in the windows, and Mike laughs, but I don't care.

The cars around us are slowing down, and when I look ahead I can see why. Two enormous roads are coming together, and all the cars in the world seem to be driving through. Buildings covered in posters and lights stretch up and up, and the sidewalks are so thick with people I can't even see the sidewalks. The air is filled with the smell of exhaust, which makes me splutter and cough. We've got cars in Warren, but not enough to fill the street with grey smoke.

'This is Times Square,' says Mike. 'And that is a subway station.' He points at a set of stairs leading down beneath the ground, and I can hear the rumble of the deep-down train coming up at me. 'They'll take you all over the city, if you know how to use them right.'

I know he is teasing and I should be mad, but I am too busy looking at Times Square to care. I think my eyes will burst trying to look at everything all at once. The Picture Shows advertised in lights, the posters for Cavalcade and Macy's and Admiral Television Appliances. Women in fancy fur coats walking through the street, their hands heavy with bright paper bags from the department stores, and hatboxes held shut with colored twine. Men in blue and brown suits tipping their hats as the ladies pass.

And the sound. The city seems to be a drum beat. Honking horns, the clatter of carts rolling by and the chorus of the vendors selling pretzels and hotdogs and hot roasted peanuts that smell like summertime. It wiggles inside my ears and travels down to my toes, making my feet hip and hop along the floor of the cart. Tapping along to the beat of the street, dancing the City. Everything is fast and loud, and I love it all.

My heart spins inside me, leaping like the ballerina I'm going to be. I will be back in New York City in no time flat. One day my name will be lit up in lights.

Mike drops me off at the corner.

'Go straight down that road and don't let anyone push you onto the subway,' he says, winking at me. 'You're supposed to pay for that, too, you know.'

I scowl, but I don't really mean it. I say thank you for the tour, and then I give him one of Mama's dimes. I want to give him the whole ten cents, but he insists on giving me a nickel change. 'A deal is a deal,' he says.

I wave goodbye to Mike, and watch him whistle his horse and cart away. Then I turn and walk up the street in the direction he showed me. All along the sidewalk, hot puffs of smelly steam burst up through metal grates, and I can hear the subway rumbling beneath my feet. My stomach flips thinking about the thousands of people under there, racing across the City underground. I walk carefully around each grate, just in case I might fall through. I don't think I'd like being that far away from the sun again; it would make me feel pinched in and nervous.

But I don't feel nervous now. I can see the numbers on the buildings, counting down to The School of American Ballet. I'm only ten buildings away, then eight, then six. My feet dance beneath me with glee. I'm almost there. Five buildings left. The world seems to slow down as I move faster, people slipping by me like in a dream. Four.

It is a dream, all of it, but it isn't. I'm really here.

Three. Two. One.

Casey Quinn has arrived.

Chapter Twelve

I am an hour early when I burst through the doors of the ballet studio. So are a lot of girls. I've never been inside Vicky's Ballet Studio, but I bet this is ten times as grand. The lobby is bigger than Vicky's whole building. And it is full of other girls in pink ballet gear, stretching their legs and pointing their toes and practicing perfect spins in front of a marble wall so shiny it could be a mirror. It seems like every girl in New York is here.

The floor in the lobby is clean white marble, and there are pictures of beautiful dancers hanging on the walls, leaping through the air like they've never heard of gravity. I crane my head back to look at the ceiling. It is higher than high, it must be miles up, and the sound of all of the girls getting ready echoes back and forth. For a moment, I feel very alone. So many girls. The ballet can't possibly take us all, and we're just the early ones.

Then I take a breath. I sit down on a bench and fold my arms. I will not be intimidated. I am one Casey Quinn. I was born to dance and I did not come all the way from Warren, South Carolina, to run away crying.

I take my lunch out of my bag. Mama's made me peanut butter and jelly, and it squidges inside my mouth. All around me girls are primping and preening. Some even put on lipstick, like that will impress the judges. I finish my sandwich in five greedy bites and swallow it down. I smile on the inside, because it makes me think of Mama and Gran, like they're here, cheering me on.

I'm sitting close to the big glass door at the front of the lobby, so I have plenty of time to get out of the way when I see Miss Priss Ann-Lee and her mother come up the steps. Mrs Ryder gives Miss Priss a hug and waves good-bye as she watches her walk through the big glass door. But I don't keep watching after that. Of all the things I don't want to deal with today, Miss Priss is number one.

I walk down the hall, past the changing room and find a small shop run by the school. Inside the window, I can see they sell books and bags and other things about ballet. There are also tights and leotards. And shoes. There, right in the window, is a brand-new perfect pair of ballet slippers. Creamy pink leather with split soles. I sigh as I press my nose to the glass, fogging the window.

'They're pretty nice,' a voice says. Standing next to me is a girl with frizzy brown hair and blue eyes. 'I'm Lily,' she says, and her smile is warm.

'I'm Casey,' I say.

'That's an unusual name.' I start to get angry, but then she says, 'It will be great when you are famous. Actually, my name is really Andrea, but that's too boring for a ballerina. I thought I'd try Lily today, but I can't really get used to it.'

'I think Andrea is a nice name.'

'That's the problem. No one remembers a nice name. I want a famous name.' She sighs dramatically, like an actress. Then she smiles. 'Are you here by yourself?'

'Yeah.'

'Me, too.' Andrea takes my arm. She just slips her hand into the crook of my elbow. No one's ever done that before, and it feels a little strange. But Andrea doesn't seem to notice and just steers me toward the changing room, talking to me about other auditions she's been to, like we've been friends all our lives. It is good to have a friend here. I don't need one, but it's nice.

The changing room is so full it is hard to move. Everywhere legs are stretching into tights, and arms flash out suddenly, as girls loop leotards over their arms. I have to duck twice to avoid being hit. The air is filled with chatter and the sound of people rushing to and fro. Andrea drags me through the room, smiling and waving to people she already knows.

'I live in a town called Monroe in upstate New York, which is, like, an hour away, but my older sister lives in the City, so I can stay with her when I audition. Where are you from?'

'South Carolina.'

'Wow, that's miles! And you came all by yourself? You are so brave. Hey, wait here, I'll be right back,' she says, and disappears back into the crowd.

The peanut butter and jelly sandwich gurgles in my stomach. I look around quickly before pulling my leotard out of the bag, but I can't see Miss Priss anywhere.

As I put on my leotard, I can't help thinking about those perfect ballet slippers and how much I wish I could buy them. I am imagining myself wearing them, and wiping the smirk off Miss Priss's face, when Andrea brings over two girls she wants me to meet. They are Julia and Chelsea, and they're from upstate New York, too.

I feel shy in my homemade costume. These girls have what Gran would call natural beauty. Even in their plain audition clothes, they look like royalty. Next to them all I have are freckles. But Andrea says my outfit looks amazing, and Julia makes me spin around. I blush, and laugh. It's a strange feeling, light and easy. No one here knows me. They don't know I live down the road past where the sidewalk stops, or that my mama and my gran work cleaning the hospital. All they know is that I want to be a dancer, just like them. Mama was wrong about New York City; it isn't mean at all.

'I can't believe you actually came.' The sound of her voice cuts me raw.

When I stop spinning I see Miss Priss staring at me. I open my mouth, but Andrea beats me to it.

'What's it to you, nosebleed?' she says. 'Why shouldn't she be here? It's an open audition.'

The other girls fold their arms and raise their eyebrows. Suddenly I am the one with a gang, and Miss Priss Ann-Lee looks very alone without Sally or Beth to stand behind her back telling her she's the best.

I look at Miss Priss. If I was in her spot, I'd stand my ground. I never back down, that's not my style. Not Miss Priss, though. She doesn't have the guts. She opens her mouth, shuts it and walks away without making a sound.

'Did you see her shoes?' whispers Andrea. 'Brand new.' The other girls nod like new shoes are bad news.

'What's wrong with new shoes?' I ask.

'Only total actors wear brand-new shoes to an audition. It's the first thing they look for.'

I think Andrea must have been to a lot of auditions. She seems to know everything. I look down at my feet and Miss Priss's hand-me-down shoes, and for the first time they don't look so bad at all.

There is a sharp knock on the changing-room door. A tall, thin woman in a black leotard steps into the room. Her arms are full of papers.

'Good morning, ladies,' she says. 'Please fill out these forms. When you're done, return them to me. I will give you your number, and you can line up outside the audition room.'

Andrea scrambles to the front of the crowd and grabs forms for both of us. She hands me mine, and a pen.

'Always be prepared,' she says, and flops down on the floor to fill her paper in.

I look at the form. 'Name'. 'Age'. 'Address'. All of the questions are simple until the last one. It says 'Previous Training'. I look around the room. The rest of the girls are all busy scribbling their own answers. I can see Miss Priss in the corner. I bet she's smirking at me. Even Andrea is too busy filling in all the places she's had lessons to notice that my page is blank.

I take a deep breath. Then I write in big, bold letters

'NONE'. And I march my paper up to the woman in the leotard without looking back. She gives me a number to pin to the front of my leotard, and writes it down on my form. I am number 53. It isn't really a lucky number, but it's not unlucky, either.

I take my number and pin it on. Andrea stands next to me.

'Is my number straight?' Andrea asks me with her hands on her hips. The square of paper across her back reads 18. I nod.

'Good,' she says and turns me around. 'Yours is, too.'

She takes my arm again and we stand outside the wooden doors, waiting. The hall behind us fills up quickly. Everyone shuffling around, nervously waiting for the audition to begin. Suddenly a path opens up through the crowd and I see the woman in the black leotard glide to the front of the group. She smiles at us all and slowly opens the doors to the audition room.

We all stand still, very still, until a voice raps out from inside the room.

'Whenever you're ready, ladies.'

My heart leaps, spinning in mid-air. The crowd pushes forward. It's time to start.

Chapter Thirteen

At first, I think there are hundreds of girls in the room. Everywhere I look is a sea of pink legs and bare arms. Then I see that the walls are lined with mirrors and ballet *barres*. It takes me a long time to find my reflection since we're all dressed in the same pink. But there I am, mug-handle ears and all. I almost look pretty in my princess dress.

We all shuffle forward, stepping slowly and dragging our feet in time to each other's nerves. I can feel it now. Everyone is so nervous it's making my bones jangle. I'm glad Mama and Gran aren't waiting on me right outside the door so close I could hear them breathing.

There is a large piano and nothing else in the room. Two men stand hunched over the keys, talking in low voices. They don't look up, but I can tell they're talking about us. Picking out the good ones.

Andrea grabs my arm and pulls me close.

'That's Mr Balanchine,' she whispers, her voice high and excited. 'He started the school. He's amazing.'

Suddenly I feel very nervous. The owner of the whole school is going to be watching us. He looks very serious sitting at the piano with his clipboard, ready to write down notes about how well we do. Or how badly.

'You OK?' Andrea asks.

I nod and swallow hard.

'You'll do great,' she says, and gives my hand a squeeze. My palm is sweaty, but I'm too busy watching the men at the piano to care.

The other man stands up and claps his hands.

'OK, ladies,' he says loudly. 'Find a spot on the barre and we'll begin.'

I know from watching classes at Miss Vicky's that you always start on the long bar bolted to the wall. I move to the edge of the room, but Andrea stops me.

'Not there. In the middle. That way you can see every-one else.'

Andrea takes her place at the very center of the barre, and I stand behind her. By looking in the mirror I can see Miss Priss in her new shoes. She is standing tall with her toes pointing out. So are a lot of the other girls. I wiggle my feet out and hold the *barre* for balance.

'All right ladies. We'll start with *pliés* in first position: two *demi-pliés*, one *grand plié*. *Relevé*. Balance. *Plié*. *Tendu* to second position. The same in second, and repeat on the other side. Ready? Prepare two measures, and begin.'

The words spill out of his mouth faster than my ears can catch them. Everyone else is nodding, shimmying themselves up to the bar. I fumble forward, copying them, my heart racing. I thought he would show us the moves, not just spit them out like old chaw. What kind of dance comes from the mouth? I dance from my soul.

The man nods his head at the piano player, and music fills the room. Beautiful, floating music. I relax. I feel my heart swell until I have to stand up straight to make room. I want to leap and sway, but no one else is moving so I stay put. Then, all at once, the entire room bends its knees. And so do I. I can see Andrea in the mirror behind me, and it is easy to move when she moves.

But I only look to make sure. I don't need to look at all. The music is telling me what to do, filling me up and carrying me along. Down and up, and down and up, with my arm floating feather-light at my side. Deep down and up on my toes. A few girls wobble, because they are just standing on their toes. They aren't reaching for the sky like me. Their legs aren't growing roots. I could stay up here forever.

The second side is easier because this time I know what to do. Miss Priss Ann-Lee is in front of me now, and when we go up on our toes she doesn't wobble at all. On the mirror her face looks different, happy, like she understands the music. But that's not possible. Miss Priss wouldn't understand music even if it was singing just for her.

We do more exercises at the bar, and each one gets a little easier. The racing rhythm of the man's words starts to take a shape and make sense. When we are done at the bar, we break up into groups. Andrea pulls me into the third group so we can watch the others first.

'Two échappés. Four changements. Three glissades right. Plié. Hold for three. Repeat other side.'

The first group steps to the middle of the floor and the music starts, a loud up-and-down beat. I know before they even start to move that it will be jumps. I am right. They spring from their knees with pointed feet and land soft like cats. Behind them, the rest of us shuffled back and forth, memorizing each move with our feet. By the time it is my turn I can touch the sky and glide over the ground like it is ice.

As I soar I smile the only smile in the whole room

because I am not just jumping up and down. I'm not just leaping gracefully. I am dancing with every inch of my body, from my toes up to my head and back down to my heart. Not even gravity can hold me down. The man looks at me and scowls. Maybe ballerinas aren't supposed to smile, but when I stop he winks, and my smile creeps back up bigger than ever.

'We'll do *pirouettes* now. First group. Fifth position. *Tendu* front to fourth. *Pirouette en dehors*, end in fourth and *tendu* close. *Tendu* to switch sides. Hold. *Repetté*.'

A rich waltz fills the room, and I sway as I watch the others. They lunge forward gently and then whoosh up with the music, spinning on one foot. Almost all of the girls wobble, because they don't let the music carry them. They're trying to dance with their brains.

Only one girl is really dancing up there. Her arms floating on the song and her legs spinning without a single doubt, as if they'd been born to dance. I almost swallow my tongue and spit out my toes when she turns around. It is Miss Priss Ann-Lee Ryder doing those perfect *pirouettes*. I can't believe it. If I had time I would wonder if she'd made a pact with the devil, but I don't have time.

The music starts again and I wait for the swell that will lift me into my spin. Then I am up and twirling. Pink figures fly past me as I spin. They swirl into thick stripes, twisting and turning and making my eyes cross. I am going too fast, almost around the world, and when I put my foot down, the room is still spinning.

I cannot hear the music above the jangling colors and when I try to do the second spin my foot gets caught behind my knee. I stumble. I'm no longer graceful. I am all chicken-leg and elbow with too-big ears and laughing Miss Priss's hand-me-down shoes.

The music stops. My face flushes red, and I bite my lip. How could I mess this up? I was born dancing. I can spin round the moon. So what was the problem with this little room?

'You forgot to spot,' says Andrea as we walk back to the wall. 'I did that at my first audition, too. Don't worry. You'll do better next time.'

I try to smile, but I can't. I'm too busy not crying.

The man at the front of the room claps his hands again. 'Alright, ladies, we will take a short break now. The names of the girls who have made the second round will be posted on the door when we've made our decision. Thank you.'

The whole room pushes together through the doors, and I lose Andrea in the crowd, but I don't care. My heart is pounding and I'm holding back tears. Outside everyone is waiting for them to post the results, whispering to each other in small clusters. The air is hot and sticky and makes my head spin like I'm losing control all over again. I lean heavily against the wall, my shoulders pressed against the cold marble.

I stay there until the woman in the black leotard appears, holding in her hand a single sheet of paper. A shiver runs through the room as she pins them to the door, and then, in a flash, everyone pushes forward, searching for their name.

Everyone except me.

Chapter Fourteen

I wait until almost all the other girls have looked at the list pinned to the door before I can go near it. My legs feel like they've turned to stone. But I force them up and down and over. I've come all the way to New York City, and I'm not going to stop here. There are a few other girls like me, waiting. I can tell they haven't done well. Their faces look thin and long, like used-up water rushing down a drain.

The names are written in small, neat letters. I can feel my heart slow beat to beat as I look for mine. But it isn't there.

I look again, running my finger up and down the list. I see Andrea's name, and the horrible words Ann-Lee Ryder, but Casey Quinn just isn't there. The floor seems to open up beneath my feet, and I feel everything spinning away from me.

I grind my toes into the floor, pushing down until everything spins back into place. It is not fair. I was born to dance. I won't let anyone stop me, and I refuse to let them get me down. A tear splashes on the toe of my shoe. I rip it off.

Anger, sharp and hot like acid, eats up my insides, and I walk back to the changing room. How could they not pick me? I am meant to be here. I know I am. And no one can tell me different.

I sit by myself on a bench in the back of the changing room and try not to cry. If I cried it would be letting them win, saying I didn't get in. So I won't cry. I'm still in New York. I've still got my feet. There's still a chance.

Other girls start to file into the changing room. Some of them have long faces and walk slowly, and I know they're the ones who didn't get called back. Like me. They get changed quickly and leave without a word. The other girls are all smiles and skipping. They run around the changing room, instantly friends with all the other chosen ones, laughing with each other, as they get ready for the next audition round.

I hunch my shoulders and stare at the floor. They don't even notice me. They're too happy for themselves, and too nervous about the next part of the audition to care about a non-ballerina like me. Tears start to leak out of my eyes. I pinch my leg savagely to stop them, but it doesn't help. I can hear footsteps, and I know it's Miss Priss coming to gloat. Swaying and swaggering in her brand-new slippers. I grit my teeth like a shield around my heart.

'Did you really think you'd get in?' Miss Priss stands over me like a vulture. I glare at her because I'm no set of dried-out bones. Not now, not ever. And I won't have her picking at me.

'You are so stuck-up. You walk around Warren like you're the only one who can dance. Like you're already too good for Vicky's Ballet Studio,' she says. Her hands are on her hips.

My mouth goes open. Miss Priss calling me stuck-up? It is almost funny, but I don't laugh. She keeps walking closer to me.

'You think you're special just because you're poor,' she says. 'Like that means you deserve to get in more than I do. Just because your father fought in the war and mine didn't.'

'What are you talking about?' I say. I'm confused.

'You've thought you were better than me ever since I came to Warren. But you're not. You don't know anything about what it means to be a ballerina. I've been taking lessons since I was four. I practice every day.'

'I practice, too,' I say.

Miss Priss tears off her brand-new shoes. 'Show me your feet,' she says.

'What?'

'Look at my feet,' she demands.

I don't want to do what she says, but I can't help it. She shoves her foot onto the bench next to me. They are disgusting. Her toenails are black and bruised. Her toes are covered with blisters and scabs. And her feet are horribly bent.

'I practice every day until my feet bleed. I want to be the best. I work really hard. I work until it hurts, and you,' her voice cracks, '. . . and you just show up, no work at all. And you think I'm the one who should go home.' Miss Priss's eyes glisten like she's going to cry. She takes a deep breath to keep the tears in. 'You think I should go home and you should stay,' she says. 'How can you even start to think that that's right?'

I stare down at the floor. My own feet stare back at me. They are long and straight with clean, healthy toenails. Not one bruise or blister in sight. I try to say something, but the words get choked back. My eyes are hot with uncried tears. Why is she saying this to me? I didn't get in. Why can't she be happy with that?

'Just leave me alone.' I force the words past the lump in my throat.

My skin feels sticky and hot with her gloating. Miss Priss looks at me like my bones aren't even worth picking at anymore. Then she shrugs and walks away.

I swallow hard at the lump in my throat, trying to force it down. I didn't get in. I got all the way to New York City, all the way from Warren, and now I have to go back. I get busy in my bag, pulling on my street shoes and blue striped traveling dress right over the top of everything else. The tights and leotard itch, but I can't take them off. Not just yet. Andrea springs into the seat next to me. Her face is red and excited.

'Did you see that? I actually made the next round!' I try to smile because Gran would say I should be gracious, but Andrea can see I'm sad. Her smile slips south. 'Don't worry about it, Casey. I didn't make my first audition, either. You'll get it next time.'

The words next time burn like iodine on a skinned knee. I don't think I'll get a next time. This was my chance. And I blew it. I'll never get to see Times Square at night, and I'll never see my name in lights.

The door to the changing room swings open and the long, thin woman from the audition steps inside. Everyone turns to look at her.

'Which one of you girls is number 53?'

My heart leaps up. Maybe she's come to say there's been a mistake. Maybe I'm already in and I don't need to go to the next audition. Maybe that was why I wasn't on the list. I swallow hard and stuff my hope back into my shoes where it belongs.

Andrea gives me a shove and I step forward as brave as I can.

'I'm number 53.'

'Mr Balanchine would like to see you,' says the woman.

Suddenly, I wonder if I'm in trouble. Maybe he's mad that I came without having had a lesson, but who is he to be mad? I was meant to be here.

I set my shoulders firmly on top of my spine and follow the long, thin woman out the dressing room. I glance over my shoulder just before I get out the door. The last thing I see is Andrea grinning and holding up her thumbs. I smile, and then I go to see Mr Balanchine. If he thinks he can just send me home, he's got another think coming. I didn't dance myself all the way to New York City to go home without a fight.

Chapter Fifteen

I storm into the empty audition room nothing like a ballerina, slapping my feet down without even trying to keep them quiet. Mr Balanchine is standing there, waiting for me. He smiles. I pull the nastiest scowl I can manage without being rude. I'm no pushover. I'm here and I mean business. Mr Balanchine looks at me standing like a soldier in front of him. Then he looks at his clipboard.

'So you are Casey Quinn,' he says. His voice has a rich foreign accent that sits at the back of his throat. I hadn't really noticed it before. I was too busy trying to understand all of the dance words. The R's roll around in his mouth now, and he clucks his tongue disapprovingly.

I let him look at me without flinching. I know what

he's looking at. He's looking at my toes poking through the holes in my tights and my scrawny legs. He's thinking, *This child is no ballerina.* I stand up tall and put my feet in first position, just to show him he doesn't know a thing.

'Is it true what you have written here?' He taps his finger on the clipboard. He's looking at the form I filled out when I arrived. 'Have you really never had a ballet lesson before?'

I stick out my chin. 'Yes, sir.'

'Have you ever had any formal dance training?'

'No, sir.'

He takes a deep breath. Then he looks at me, really looks at me like I am a book and he is reading me. I try not to twitch as the seconds tick by. This is a test, I tell myself. He's watching for something. Suddenly, Mr Balanchine lets the breath out in a whoosh.

'Well, then you are a natural dancer,' he says.

'Then why didn't I get in?' The words are out before I can stop them, but he doesn't seem to mind.

'You don't have enough technical training. If you'd come a few years ago when we were just starting I would have trained you myself. But now . . .' He makes the little shrug with his shoulders that grown-ups make when they want to say, *It's not my fault.*

'You can either go home and take a few years of

lessons, or . . .' he holds up his hands before I can interrupt and say I don't have money for lessons, 'or, there is something else.'

He takes a piece of paper and writes something down. 'There is another audition in two months. It is not a ballet school. It is a different type of dance, but I think it will suit you very well. And . . .' he pauses, 'I think you will like it. When are you going home?'

'My bus is at six.'

'Good,' he says. 'Take this note to the studio on 316 East 63rd Street. Just between First and Second. Can you get there?'

I nod. Now I've seen the street system, it isn't so hard. The street and avenue numbers all go in order, and I can count just fine.

He puts the piece of paper in my hands. 'Don't ever stop dancing, Casey Quinn. You have a great gift. You either go to her, or come back to me in a few years. Now, hurry up or you will miss the class.'

Most of the girls are gone when I get back to the changing room. They've started the next stage of the audition. As I pull on my high-tops and grab my bag, I notice a note tucked inside it. It is from Andrea. It says 'Good Luck'. Her address is written on the back. I stare at it for a moment, not sure exactly what to do.

It seemed so easy for Andrea to decide we'd be friends, like she made new ones all the time. I wonder if she'd still want to be my friend if she knew more about me. Then I remember how she took on Miss Priss, and I smile. I take a deep breath and I pull my crumpled number 53 out of my bag and write 'You too!' on the back and my address, and tuck it into Andrea's street shoes. Today is a day for taking chances.

I walk out onto the street and I smile. I really hope she gets in.

I eat the rest of the lunch Mama packed me as I soar down the sidewalk, skipping in my high-tops. Hope lifting me up at every turn.

I watch where I'm going this time, and steer well clear of the subway steps.

I arrive at the dance studio fifteen minutes later. It's a dark little hall, with stairs leading up behind the front desk. Very different from The School of American Ballet, but there is a buzz in the air that reminds me of the city, fast and exciting. The woman at the desk frowns at me at first, but when I hand her the note her face opens.

'Come with me,' she says, and I follow her upstairs.

Strange, pulsing music is pouring out of the walls. I've never heard anything like it. One, two, three. One, two-three. One-two, three. The beat shifts from one count to the next without taking a breath.

At the top of the stairs is a large room filled with dancers. They are striding, knees bent low to the ground, straight-backed. Another group is standing to the side, waiting for their turn. And in the middle of the room is the most amazing woman I have ever seen. She is tall, larger than herself somehow. Like her spirit is too big for her body. Little bits seem to pour out every time she moves. The air bends around her as she prowls between the dancers.

'Stop!' She claps her hands, and the room is silent and still.

'You're missing it. Push off on one, stay in the air on two. Listen to the music. Again.'

The music starts again and I move my feet without moving. I want to feel how those dancers look, like I'm flying. They go around the room again. Then the woman claps once more, and they stop.

'We've run over. That is all for today. Thank you.'

As the dancers file out, the other woman, the one from the front desk, leads me into the room.

'Martha,' she says to the teacher. 'This girl wants to audition for the scholarship program.'

Miss Martha looks down at me. 'That isn't for two more months.'

Somehow I find my voice. 'I know, ma'am,' I say, pulling the words from the back of my throat. 'But I was at the ballet audition and Mr Balanchine said I should come here. So I came here.'

The other woman hands Miss Martha the note.

I hesitate. Then I say, 'What kind of dance do you teach? I've never seen it before.'

She arches one eyebrow without looking up from the paper.

'A new way to move,' she says. Other dancers are coming into the room for the next class. They don't even look at me. They're too busy getting ready.

'I like it,' I say.

She looks at me, first my face and then my body, like she's looking for a lie. But I'm not lying. Those dancers danced right out from their insides.

'Well then,' she says. 'You may sit in the back row and learn something today, and come back for the audition in two months.'

I struggle out of my shift, glad that I left my tights and leotard on underneath it. All of the other dancers have bare feet, so I make a hole in the toe of my tights and rip it until my whole foot fits through.

'Bounces,' says Miss Martha, and the piano starts to play.

Everyone sits on the floor with their knees bent and the soles of their feet together, and bobs their heads toward the floor. Then Miss Martha snaps her fingers, and everyone spreads their legs out to the side and keeps bobbing. Another snap, another position.

People are curling up on the floor and springing loose. Standing and falling and rising from the earth.

'Don't just go through the motions,' Miss Martha yells at us. 'At all times, the dancer should feel poised as if in flight – even when sitting.' She looks at where I sit, and almost smiles. I think she can see it. The way I am sitting. The way I'm dancing on the inside. The way I am flying. It is like no dance in the world. It is better. I can feel each move in my gut. You could dance anger like this. Not just the way anger looks or feels, but the anger itself. Or joy, or sadness, or anything.

It is like I am watching their bodies talk and mine wants to talk, too. And it doesn't matter that my legs are too skinny or I have more freckles on my face than there are stars in the sky. It doesn't matter that my ears stick out, not one bit. Because this is my kind of dance. It is already inside me, and no one can take it away. This is where I am meant to be.

Miss Martha claps her hands again and tells us the lesson is over. The other dancers move to the sides of the room, pulling on their over-clothes and shoes, and filing out of the room through the small wooden doorway. They are laughing and talking with one another, and I follow them quietly.

I feel a hand clamp down on my shoulder and spin me around.

'Now, show me what you've learnt,' Miss Martha says, waving me to the middle of the room.

My heart trills like a songbird, but when the music starts I take a breath and let it carry me. It sweeps through my body like it is talking to me, and I dance my answers all the way to my fingertips.

'Alright, that's enough.' Miss Martha stops me.

My heart leaps up into my mouth and I have to swallow it back down again as I stare into Miss Martha's eyes, black like the middle of the night. She stares right back at me, and I go all cold as if she's looking through me.

It seems like forever before she speaks.

'Very good,' she says. 'I will see you in two months for the audition. You have promise.'

Then she is gone.

I walk out of Miss Martha's studio and down the street, floating toward the bus station. I don't care if people push past me, or shoot me the greasy eyeball for not scooting fast enough. I want to soak up every last second of the city.

I breathe the air deep, trying to memorize the smell. I know I'll be back, but I want something to hold onto, something to remember while I'm waiting in the wings in Warren.

When I get on the bus to go home, my heart is full and I am twitching all over to try my new moves. Gran would say that I've reached for the stars and landed on the moon. But I think it's the other way round. I think this is how Mama must have felt when she was painting my room. I can't imagine ever giving this up. I think Mama must have been real sad to stop painting.

There is no one in the seat next to me, so I stretch out. With my face up, I can look out the bus window into the sky. The sun goes down slowly, and the sky is peachy pink, a celebration. It melts slowly into darkness, first purple and then navy. And one by one the stars pop out, bright silver dots that light up the night sky, twinkling just like I imagine the lights in Times Square must twinkle.

I lie there as the bus carries me through the night. And I don't mind that it's taking me back to Warren. I have something new to reach for. Maybe you can't do ballet in high-tops, but that don't mean you can't dance. I look at the papers Miss Martha's assistant gave me, running my fingers over the magical words: 'The Martha Graham School of Contemporary Dance'. My school.

Chapter Sixteen

It is just afternoon when the bus gets back. I expect Mama to be there, but she isn't. She must be working another emergency shift at the hospital.

I am humming into my fingertips as I run down the empty street. Warren is quiet and still and so small compared to New York City. I feel like a giant stepping through the dusty streets. One, two, three. With a leap up on the two. My high-tops drum out my happiness.

Our house is empty when I burst inside. I walk about, twitching to tell someone about my adventure. I check all the rooms, but Mama and Gran aren't anywhere. It is strange that Gran is out. She must be at the hospital, too. I sit at the table and wait. My fingers dance impatiently over the table top, itching to tell Mama and Gran my good news. The sun begins to wink down toward the horizon, and I have no sleep in my bones. I put some water on the stove for when Mama and Gran come home. Then I sit at the table to wait.

When I wake up, the water is off the stove and Mama is sitting across the table watching me.

'Casey,' she begins, and I sit up with a start.

'I'm sorry I left the water on, Mama. I wanted to surprise you for when you came home. And I didn't think I was tired.' The words spill out of me like music. 'Oh Mama, I didn't get into the ballet school, but it's OK. There's a new school, a better school.'

'Casey . . .' Mama says it like she hasn't slept for days.

'But Mama, it's true. And if I go back in two months there's a scholarship audition.'

'Casey!' Mama bangs her hand on the table. Then she starts crying.

I pull my breath back into my body. Something is wrong. Mama cries like a runaway train tearing down a mountain. Her huge sobs gain speed until she stops them all, crashing her fists against her thighs and roaring at herself with a tight, strangled growl.

My heart beats a deep booming in my hollow chest. Something is wrong.

'Mama,' I ask softly. 'Where's Gran?'

Mama's breath catches, and I see her pinch her leg to keep from crying, just the way I do. 'Gran is in the hospital.'

She says 'in' not 'at' – and that one little word brings down the sky.

'Gran's had a heart attack.' Mama starts to cry again. I am still for a moment before I get out of my chair and put my arms around her. She sobs into my shoulder and my neck.

'I don't want my mama to die,' she says.

'Gran won't die. You'll see,' I say as I rock her back and forth, because Gran can't die. Gran is too alive to die.

But Mama keeps on crying, clinging to me like I am a rock in a fast-moving stream, like I am the mama. I hold her until she stops crying. Then I make her some tea and carry it to her bedroom. Mama lies in her bed, but she doesn't drink her tea and she doesn't sleep. She just looks white and worried.

I sit on my own bed with my knees pulled up to my chest. I feel very small and too big for my skin all at the same time. I never realized how much Mama loves Gran. And when I think about that, I realize that I don't know how much I love Mama. That love is big, like an endless lake sparkling so bright in the sun that it hurts even to look at it. That is my love for Gran, too. I get up and look in the mirror. How can such a scrawny body hold so much feeling inside it?

I never knew my father. Not really. He left for the war before I could remember more than crawling by his feet. In fact, the only thing I remember about my father is his shoes. Chuck Taylor high-tops, just like mine. The official shoe of the army. I wonder if I'd had him for longer whether my love would be divided up more, but I don't think so. I think we stretch out forever in our hearts, just like the water on my wall.

In the morning, when Mama wakes up, we go to the hospital to see Gran. I fight to remember that I was there just a few days ago, dancing with a broom in time to the beeping machines. They don't sound so musical now.

We go down a long white hall to a small room with a smaller window high in its wall. There is a bed in the middle of the room, but it isn't Gran in the bed. It can't be. Gran is large and always moving. She has wobbly arms that shake when she laughs or mashes potatoes. She smells like warm bread and love, and she vibrates with life.

The woman in the bed just lies there. She's not awake, but she's not dreaming either. Long wires go from her skin and attach to a small machine by her bed. But it is Gran.

Mama and I hold hands as we walk to the bed. Gran fills it up, but she doesn't fill up herself. She looks light, like she might just up and float away.

'Hi, Gran,' I say. Mama lets go of my hand like she's going to say Gran can't hear me. But I don't let her.

'I'm back from New York City,' I say. 'I did good. I didn't get in, but I did good. The head teacher said I was a natural dancer. And he told me about a new dance school. And I went there. It was amazing, Gran. People danced with their guts. I'm going back in two months to audition there. So you'll have to come see me.' My voice cracks. I stop talking, but I think I see a smudge of a smile spread on Gran's lips.

I look up and Mama is crying again, more gently this time. I wrap my arm around her waist and squeeze gently. She squeezes me back. I squeeze again, this time with one of the beeps from the machine by Gran's bed. Mama squeezes back on the next beat. We stay hugging each other to the beat of Gran's heart until the nurse comes in and tells us we have to leave.

On the way out of the hospital, I see Mrs Ryder.

'I'm so sorry about your grandmother,' she says. 'But I'm sure she'll be fine.'

'Me, too,' I say. 'Did Ann-Lee get into the school?'

Mrs Ryder's face glows. 'She did. She's been dreaming

about dancing in New York since she was little.' Suddenly, Mrs Ryder remembers I didn't even make the first cut. She takes off her smile. 'I'm sorry you didn't make it, Casey.'

'That's OK,' I say. 'I found something else.'

As we walk out of the hospital, I wonder why I'm not more upset about Miss Priss getting in, why I'm not beating the sidewalk with angry feet. I remember the look on Miss Priss's face when she bet me she would get in and I wouldn't. And when she came to gloat because she was right. It had made me mad enough to scream, but I don't feel mad anymore. I am too full of thinking about Gran. Ann-Lee is a drop in a bucket. I wonder why I ever bothered worrying about her at all.

Mama takes my hand again, not like I'm her little girl and not like I'm her mama. It is like we are friends. And we go home and cook dinner together, waiting for tomorrow when we can visit Gran again.

Chapter Seventeen

Gran died in the night. Her heart stopped working. And when Mama tells me, my heart stops working, too. It beats, pumping blood up and down, but that is all it does. It doesn't feel, and I don't cry. Mama is awash in tears, but I am bone dry. I am too empty for tears. I am too empty for anything except a low dull ache at the back of my eyes.

Mama stays in bed so I cook dinner: soup with vegetables and no chicken fat. I've thrown out the butter and sour cream and all the things Gran used to cook, used to cook. But I don't cry. I've gotta be strong for Mama.

When the hospital calls about what to do with Gran's body, I tell Mama I'm going for a walk. At the hospital, Mrs Ryder says she will help me with the funeral arrangements. She says she is sorry and I say thank you, but I don't really mean it. I don't really believe that Gran is dead. How could she be? How could Gran, who always knew what to say, die? How could the Cakewalk Queen die?

The funeral is on a Thursday. Mama is a little better. She makes me put on the old black dress and pinchy patent-leather shoes Mrs Ryder sent over. I don't want to wear them. I don't care that they're Ann-Lee's. I just don't want to wear them because wearing black is like admitting defeat. But when I look at Mama's red eyes, I shut my mouth and squeeze in my feet.

The cemetery is full of Warren. All dressed in black and tipping their hats to pay their respects. Everyone seems to have a story about her. 'Your gran,' they say as they smile at me. And I know they mean it kindly. But every time they say it, it pinches at my soul, just like Ann-Lee Ryder's shoes are pinching at my feet, making my toes cramp.

I want them to go away. She is my gran, not theirs. They weren't there with her like Mama and me. They didn't know her, not really, no matter what stories they tell. Mama is crying, and I want to cover her ears and take her away and yell at the rest of them that Gran is not dead. Even when they lower the coffin into the ground I don't believe it. Gran couldn't fit into that box. Gran is the whole world.

Mr and Mrs Ryder drive Mama and me home. Mama's eyes are pink, but they're dry. Ann-Lee sits fidgeting in the seat next to me. She is much smaller than I remember. She offers me a lemon drop. I look at her. I want to say congratulations for getting into the ballet school. I mean it, too, and that surprises me. But I can't. Not yet. Instead, I take the lemon drop and say thank you as nicely as I can.

Mrs Ryder wanted us to come back to their house after the funeral where everyone could say they were sorry and feed us comfort food. But I said no. I don't think Mama or me will ever get comfort from eating again. Great helpings of chicken and potatoes will always remind me too much of Gran. Instead I just ask the Ryders to take us home.

The first thing I do is kick off Ann-Lee's too-tight shoes. I flick them angrily across the kitchen and tear off the itchy black dress after them. Gran is not dead and I'm not in mourning. Mama turns to look at me – standing in the middle of the kitchen just wearing my underwear – and suddenly her face cracks open and I see her smile. I smile, too. We're going to be OK, Mama and me.

Two days later, I walk in on Mama opening the mail. Reading the cards that make her sad all over again. 'I'm

Sorry', they say, and 'With Deepest Sympathy'. I wish people would stop sending them. Mama pulls a plain envelope out of the pile and opens it with shaky hands. Then Mama is falling, crunching in at the stomach and crumpling at the knees. It reminds me of the dancers in Miss Martha's class. Only Mama doesn't spring up from the floor. She just sits there crying without making a sound or shedding a tear.

I pick up the paper she was reading. It is a bill from the hospital for Gran's stay. Just one sheet of paper and not even a note saying 'We're sorry we couldn't save her'.

The next day, I am back at work cleaning the recovery ward. I don't dance my broom dance. I just sweep and empty the trashcans into the big bin at the end of the hall. I don't go to the janitor's office unless I have to, because I always see Gran sitting there, resting her feet on her bucket and drinking her cup of coffee.

Mama is back at work, too, because the bill for Gran is expensive. I bet Gran would be real mad if she knew, but that hurts too much to think about. I wish I could stop school and just work. I want to help Mama pay the bill, because owing the money is like having Gran die again every day. But Mama won't even let me talk about quitting school.

I'm glad when people stop asking how we are doing. I

am tired of lying. I feel numb inside when Miss Priss brags about her big City plans for next year, Sally and Beth hanging on every word. They always drop their voices low when I walk by, like they're worried I might break if I hear them. But I am too tired to care.

It is all sweep, eat, sweep, sleep for me and Mama. It is a rhythm, but it's not a dance. Nothing is a dance anymore.

It is a month and two weeks exactly after we buried Gran. I walk home from the hospital slowly, tired and hollow. Each step thuds against the side of the road. Mama is waiting for me at home. She works the night shift most days now. It pays more, but it means we only see each other for about an hour at dinner. Two ships passing in the night, Mama calls us.

Today Mama is sitting at the kitchen table with an old shoebox and a stack of papers. Her face is dry, but I can see where her tears have left two salty tracks along her cheeks.

'Sit down, Casey,' Mama says. I pull up a seat.

Mama pushes the shoebox toward me. It is full of money, full like a treasure chest, full of dimes and nickels and quarters and rolled-up dollar bills neatly wrapped together with kitchen twine. I look at Mama, my mouth open wide. There must be a hundred dollars there, at least.

'Where'd you get this?' I ask.

'I started to clean out Gran's room,' Mama says quietly, staring at the table top.

'You were going through Gran's stuff?' I say angrily. That's Gran's room. No one goes in there but her.

Mama doesn't say anything. She just hands me a sheet of paper and folds her arms. It is a letter from Gran.

I always knew I wouldn't be around forever and if you're reading this it means I'm gone. I have lived a full life and I've followed my dreams and I don't have any regrets. You can't ask for more than that. This money is for Casey to follow her dreams, wherever they take her. Make sure she uses it well.

I read the letter again. And then again, just to make sure. But the letters are strong and wobbly, just like Gran. I know she really wrote it. The money is mine, but I don't want it at all.

Chapter Eighteen

The money sits between us like an accusing finger. *This is all your fault and now you have me, so I hope you're happy.*

I am not happy. I killed Gran. All those times she sneaked sweets and second helpings, and cooked with butter or fat from the can. I never said anything. Mama tried to save her, but I never helped. That's why Gran always won.

Worst of all were the mornings I had detention. I lied and told Mama Gran and I were taking a walk. She'd been so happy that Gran was exercising, and I was so worried about being in trouble and not being allowed to audition that I didn't tell her the truth. I was greedy for my dream, so greedy I forgot my family. And now the money points at me.

'You can have my money,' I say. 'That will pay the hospital bill.'

A storm passes over Mama's face. For a moment, I think she's going to slap me.

'How dare you even think that? Your gran didn't work cleaning that hospital for forty years to save this money just so you could give it right back.'

My heart leaps, because this is Mama talking, the real Mama. My no-nonsense, strict-as-nails Mama. But I still don't agree with her.

'But Mama—' I say.

'No buts, Casey. Gran said that money is for you to follow your dreams. So you better use it.'

Mama's voice is so sure that I feel myself go soft against it. And when I go soft I feel something that might be hope. But when I look at it, it's not. It's too low around the edges to be hope.

'Mama,' I say. 'I don't know if I can dance anymore.'

Mama hugs me. We hug a lot more now than we used to.

'Casey, you were born dancing. I've been trying to get you to sit still your whole life.'

I smile but I don't really mean it. All the dance went out of me when Gran died, like a snuffed candle.

'I know you're sad now, Casey, but think about Gran.' I

don't want to think about Gran. It makes the ache come back. 'Think about what she would want you to do. She wouldn't want you to spend the rest of your life cleaning the hospital.'

I want to ask, *What about you? Do you want to spend the rest of your life cleaning the hospital?* But I am too tired to argue. Mama nods. She stands up and puts the money in the cookie tin on top of the refrigerator. Then she goes to bed, and I go to school.

I'm late, but no one says anything. They just cluck and shake their heads as I walk by. I grind my teeth because I know what they're thinking. They're thinking, *Poor Casey Quinn. She's lost her grandmother. We'll give her time. She'll get over it.* But I won't. Not ever, you hear me?

I am still fuming when I get to work. I scrub the dirt like it's all those people who think they know how I feel. They don't know anything. I stalk into Mr Homes's room, silent as a flea. I wouldn't want to disturb His Majesty. Oh, no, not precious Mr Homes.

He is sitting up on his web of a bed, waiting for me. He always watches me clean, and I always ignore him.

'You're in a mood today, aren't you?' he says as I beat the dust with my broom. 'Who pickled your ears?'

It's the first time he's said anything to me since before the ballet audition. I go right on ignoring him.

'You lose your voice or something?'

I empty the dustpan into the trash.

'Well, at least I don't have to watch that infernal cake-walk you call dancing anymore.'

I slam the trashcan down and walk out of the room.

When I am in the doorway, Mr Homes says, 'Wait.'

I don't know why I turn around. He probably wants to tell me I missed a spot. I stare at him, waiting. He looks a little confused, like he's scared of my eyes.

'I'm . . .' He licks his lips. 'Your grandmother was a powerful lady,' he says. 'I'm sure you miss her.' Then he clears his throat and rolls over, turning his back to me.

I stand there, wide-eyed.

'Well, can't you see I'm trying to sleep?' he rumbles.

I take the trashcan to the bin at the end of the hall. I think that is the closest Mr Homes has ever come to saying he's sorry, to anyone. And the funny thing is, out of all the people saying things about Gran, I think that Mr Homes is the only one who even started to understand.

I wonder if he lost someone he loved as wide as the ocean, and if that is what made him so hateful. Maybe Gran knew that. I think Gran knew a lot about people. I throw the trashbag into the bin and then start for home.

I don't want to turn sour inside like Mr Homes, but I don't know how to stop it. Already I can feel my soul curdling, and every time I think about Gran it gets worse. All my trapped tears are in there like poison, but I can't let them out. Now I know why Mama is so sour sometimes. I wonder if that's why she gave up painting.

Step. Swish. Step. I sway down the sidewalk toward home, looking for an answer, and only seeing my feet.

Chapter Nineteen

I sit still and unsmiling the whole bus ride to New York. I feel unsolid and uncomfortable in my blue-and-white striped traveling dress. I am so different from who I was the last time I wore this dress. That evil worm is coiling itself inside my stomach and squeezing all of my organs into new, uncomfortable places. The only way to keep it quiet is to be very still. I spend most of the time staring out the window, but not seeing anything.

I leave Warren at night, and it is already afternoon when the man calls, 'Port Authority'. No one even looks at me as I walk toward Miss Martha's studio. I drag my feet the whole way.

I don't understand why Mama sent me here. She was right before. A person shouldn't be greedy for their dreams. Besides, even if I get in, I can't go. I can't leave Mama all by herself in dry-as-dust Warren. Just her and the hospital. She needs me.

I walk up the steps and go into the studio. The same strange, wobbling music fills the air and my heart leaps a little, but I stop it flat. It isn't right to want to dance when I don't have Gran anymore.

There are only a few other girls here, and a boy. I go to the corner and take off my top layer. I'm wearing the leotard Gran made and it itches, but it is the only one I have.

Miss Martha sweeps into the room. Her lips are painted bright red and her hair is pulled back with a white band.

'Take the floor,' she says. We spread out across the room and watch each other nervously. 'We will begin with bounces. Edith will demonstrate.'

A skinny woman with long dark hair moves to the front of the room and sits down facing us with her knees bent and the soles of her feet together. She then curves her back and bounces her head gently toward her feet.

I remember seeing the dancers stretching like this when I was here before, and as I sit down it seems like that was a very long time ago.

'Now in time with my counting,' Miss Martha says.

So I bounce. But the movement doesn't fill me up like it used to. This thing growing inside me seems to be taking up all the space.

Edith moves her legs out to the sides and keeps bouncing. I copy her.

Miss Martha stops us. 'Now we will try something more difficult. Watch Edith.'

Edith kneels next to Miss Martha. She isn't pretty like a ballet dancer, all soft lines and grace, but when she moves everyone seems to stop breathing.

Miss Martha counts to six, and with each beat Edith shifts, her body surging forward like a river breaking its banks. Her head is on the floor, her back arching until I can see the force in her legs like the high winds of a hurricane. She relaxes back and then rolls forward again, her whole body rippling and rushing like water. She is beautiful and strong, and it is frightening to look at her.

Miss Martha looks at us. 'We will try. The power comes from drawing your stomach toward your spine as you breathe out. Use your breath.'

We all kneel, and she raps out the counts with her feet.

One. I flow forward slowly, more like a gentle stream than a river in the rainy season. I want to dance like Edith, to dance out all my feelings like I used to, but it hurts too much.

Two. I place my head on the floor and breathe in the dust of the studio.

Three. Up again.

Four. Head on the floor.

Five. Breathe.

Six. Get ready to start again.

Miss Martha walks around the room, watching us all carefully. 'No, breathe out forcefully. Keep your stomach strong.' She scowls at us and roars, 'Again.'

My legs start to tremble.

'Stop!' She is standing next to me. 'What happened to you? Why aren't you dancing?'

I look up into her huge eyes. I don't want to say anything. Miss Martha waits. She isn't going to let me pretend nothing is wrong. I swallow hard. Then I say what I haven't said yet. I haven't said it to anyone. Not even to myself.

'My gran died,' I say. One fat tear, big enough to hold all the sadness I haven't cried, wiggles behind my eye.

'So?' says Miss Martha, raising one eyebrow like it is a dance all by itself. 'You shouldn't stop dancing because you are sad. You should dance more than ever. We'll do the exercise again,' she says to the class. 'And this time put some feeling into the movement. Let your body speak. One!'

I breathe out hard and roll forward and think about Gran. It hurts, but I make myself do it anyway.

Two. My neck curves as if I'm diving into murky water, and I think about her smile and her great wobbly arms and how she always believed in me.

Three. I push up, fighting against the storm. I think about her swollen ankles and how she never listened to Mama, not once.

Four. I become the river, anger and sadness flowing into my movements. Why wouldn't she listen? Why did she have to be so stubborn?

Five. Breathe.

'Six,' yells Miss Martha. 'Again!'

One. The news of Gran's death washes over me like a flood, rolling my body forward and forcing the air from my lungs.

Two. I hold onto my sadness with all my strength, arching my back until I feel I must break.

Three. I rise up as if to catch my breath until . . .

Four. The power of the river pulls me back down, tumbling over and through and all around me.

Five. I sit still, holding tight to Gran's memory.

Six. Again.

And again.

And again.

We run through the moves until my muscles are numb. I am sweaty and tired, but I keep going, driven by emotion. I finally understand how Ann-Lee danced until her feet bled. As I feel the tumble and rush of the movement, all of my sadness rises to the surface of my skin. I shut my eyes because I don't want to look. But Miss Martha yells, 'Don't shut your eyes. Shutting your eyes is cowardly and self-indulgent. Present your gaze!'

My eyes snap open as we go through the counts again. The cycle of loving Gran, and letting go, and understanding that she's gone.

When we finally stop, I am soaking wet from sweat and from tears. I am crying. Giant sobs shake my whole body and fill the room, but I don't care.

'All right,' Miss Martha says. 'That's enough.' She is talking about both my tears and the audition. I nod and dry my face. I feel very light.

No one says anything about my crying as we dress and go out to the hall to wait. No one talks to me, either, but I don't mind. I feel very separate from everything. All I want to do is to go home and see Mama.

One by one, the other dancers are called back into the room, and one by one they come back out and leave. I am called in last.

Miss Martha is sitting in a director's chair at one end of the room. She motions me over to her.

'At the end, you were dancing,' she says. 'But I will not put up with hysterics.' Her eyes are serious and they seem to be saying something, but I am too tired to read them. 'So from now on, no more breaking down, just working hard.'

I nod.

'Aren't you excited?'

I frown, because I don't know what she means.

'You got the scholarship, Miss Quinn,' she says.

For a moment I just stand there, and then I realize what she said. 'Really?'

My body fills with warmth, and a smile grows up from the soles of my feet.

'You'll start in September. Give my assistant downstairs your address and she will mail you everything you need.'

I am quiet for a long time, and then, slowly, like I am remembering myself, I say, 'Thank you.'

Miss Martha nods. She understands. It is enough.

After I give my name and address to the woman in the office, I walk outside and take a deep breath of warm evening air. I can almost taste the City in the breeze, the cars and noise, hot dogs and roast peanuts. It smells like hope.

I walk slowly back toward the bus station. My feet are light and my steps turn into skips. Small skips that are almost like dancing. Gran was right. You have to be sad, and you have to let go. And now I really do dance, with leaps and kicks and turns. I am Casey Quinn. This city hasn't seen anything yet. I've danced my dreams true, and I'm just getting started.

Chapter Twenty

I sit very still on the bus ride home, not because I am trying to quiet bad feelings and not because I am tired. I sit still because I don't need to move to dance. I am poised for flight. I did it. And no one can ever say that Casey Quinn is an awkward child ever again. They can't say I'm ugly either, because when I dance I am beauty-full of grace, even in my ratty-tatty, used-to-be-white, two-sizes-too-big Converse high-top shoes.

As the bus sways me around a curve, I hear something clink in my pocket. It is the dime Mama gave me when I first came to New York City and the nickel left over from my ride with Mike. I can't believe I forgot about them.

I look out the window of the bus like my eyes can take me back to buy something I will always remember. Then

I stop. That was when Mama thought I would never go back to New York City. When she thought I wouldn't get in. But I did get in. Maybe not into The School of American Ballet, but I got into Miss Martha's school. And Miss Martha's school is better for me. Miss Martha's school has a heart like mine. It beats right on the surface.

Maybe I should just give the money back to Mama, to help out with the bills. I don't need to buy anything now. But that doesn't seem right. Like Mama said, I don't think Gran saved it up to give it back to the hospital! No, this money is for something special. I just don't know what.

The bus arrives early. As I wait for Mama, I look around. The paint set is still in the window of Willy's General Store. I know what the money is for. It's for Mama's dream. I walk into the store, holding the coins tight in my hand.

When I come out, I see Mama walking toward me. I run to meet her. My bag is heavy with the painting set, and it bangs against my leg. I don't mind at all.

'I got in! I got in!' I yell as I leap off the sidewalk right into Mama's arms.

She hugs me fierce and smiles. 'I'm so proud of you, Casey.'

'Really?' I say as we walk home.

Mama says, 'Of course.'

After dinner, I sit in my room. Mama calls Mrs Ryder

person-to-person to see where Ann-Lee is living in New York City. I'm not so happy about the idea of living with Miss Priss. She might have worked hard to get into The School of American Ballet, but she's still too uppity and pinky-pink for me. I won't let a little thing like that stop me, though. Besides, we'll be at different dance schools.

And maybe Andrea will be in New York, too – I'm sure she'll have got into the ballet school. I have her address on my bureau, and I know how to write. It would be nice to have a friend. Someone who loves dance just like I do. I don't need one, but it would be nice.

Mama comes in to say goodnight, sitting on the edge of the bed while I crawl under the covers.

'Mrs Ryder says Ann-Lee is going to live in a boarding house for dance students and you could probably get a room there, too.'

Mama looks around my room at her painting. It hits me that I will have to leave the world Mama gave me behind.

'Mama, do you think you'll ever paint again?'

Mama looks shocked. Then she thinks about it. 'I don't know, Casey,' she says slowly. 'When your father died, my painting just dried up.'

'Don't you miss it?'

She looks at the painting again.

'Yes.' She says it with a big whoosh of air. Like she's

been waiting her whole life to let it out.

'I think you should try,' I say.

I climb back out of bed and get the paint set out of my closet and put it on Mama's knees. As I crawl back into bed, I watch Mama open the box and run her fingers over the brightly colored tubes of paint. Her face is soft and far away.

'It was really hard to dance because I was so sad about Gran, but Miss Martha made me. And the dancing made me feel better. So maybe the painting will make you feel better, too?'

Mama looks up at me. Her eyes are big and wet, but her mouth is smiling.

'Will you try?' I ask one more time.

'We'll see.' Mama kisses me on the forehead and says goodnight. Then she shuts off the light and closes the door. I think we'll see means yes.

I am full of happiness and sadness and fear all at the same time. Everything's changing so fast. The world is spinning like an out-of-control pirouette. I want it to stop but I can't even make it slow down.

I lie in bed, looking up into the darkness, and I miss my gran. But not sharp like before. It's a soft kind of miss, because I know she'd be proud of me if she were here. Her dancing baby going all the way to New York City. But if Gran is in heaven, and New York City is the stars, then maybe we won't be that far away from each other after all.

Chapter Twenty-One

I sit on the front porch, squinting over the hot red dirt and waiting for the Ryders to arrive. It is early morning, but the sun is already strong on my feet, baking my toes inside my high-tops. The rest of me is tucked up safe in the long shade of our front porch, but even without the sun on my skin it is hot. The air is so still and heavy even the flies can't be bothered to buzz around. And the ground seems to shimmer like water boiling off a hot pan.

Behind me the front door creaks open and bangs shut, and I can hear Mama walking onto the porch. She is huffing and puffing 'cause it is even hotter inside than it is out.

Mama sits down on the porch next to me and hands

me a slice of cool, fresh watermelon dripping with red juice.

'Any sign of them?' Mama asks, and I shake my head. I take a bite and the juice dribbles down my chin. On the outside I am quiet and calm but not inside. Oh, no. Inside I am lit up bright as bright can be. I'm going to New York City today to dance with Martha Graham. I spit out a watermelon seed with a little pop and watch it sail into the shimmering red dirt, a perfect arc of joy.

Mama puts her arm around my shoulder and squeezes me close.

'You all packed?'

I nod again, and swallow hard. All of my things fit snug as you please into one small suitcase. Old and faded blue with a leather strap wrapped round the outside, it is sitting on the porch behind me. It doesn't seem like much to be leaving with, but I can't take the big things with me. I hadn't thought about leaving, not really. I thought about getting out of no-good Warren all the time. But that was different. That was just imagining leaving all the bad stuff in the red Carolina dust. I never thought about all the good stuff I'd have to leave. Like my room, and Mama.

'And you've got all of the addresses and telephone numbers written down?'

'I've got everything, Mama,' I say.

'Are you sure? Let me see your bag.'

I give Mama 'The Look'.

'I know, I know. Just humor me,' she smiles. Her eyes are big and full of blue, like two giant lakes.

Mama's been making sure I have everyone's phone number written down since I got into The Martha Graham School of Contemporary Dance. She's got a list of them as long as my arm, pinned to the wall by our telephone: the boarding house, my high school, Miss Martha's office. She's even got the New York City police department's number there, just in case. I told Andrea about it in one of my letters, and she said her mother was even worse.

I sigh and open my knapsack, but I don't mind really. I show Mama the letter from Mrs Everton's Boarding House for Young Ladies saying I've got a room, and my letter from Miss Martha's school. In the address book Mama bought for me at Willy's General Store I've got our phone number, so I can call home, and the Ryders' number in case there's an emergency. I've got Andrea's New York City address in there, too. She did get into the ballet school, after all!

'And where's your class schedule for regular school?'

I just wanted to go to New York to be a dancer. But Mama wasn't having any of that. 'You'll finish high school or you won't go,' she said. So I'm enrolled in Lincoln High School, which is right near the boarding house. Miss Priss is going there, too, but so is Andrea, so maybe it won't be so bad.

Mama looks over my school schedule and nods once. She hands it back to me, and I fold all of my papers back up and put them safe and sound in my bag.

'All right, Mama?' I say.

Mama smiles a secret smile. 'I've got one more thing for you,' she says, and pulls out a skinny, square package from behind her back. 'You were right, you know,' she says softly. 'The painting does help.'

I turn over the square. It is a canvas, and Mama has painted our house on it. It winks at me from the end of a long, oak tunnel, like it is welcoming me home. It is so beautiful it makes me want to cry and smile all at the same time. We are quiet for a moment, sitting in the heat of the rising sun, thinking too many things to say.

'I am going to miss you, Casey,' Mama says. 'This house is gonna be real quiet without you.'

'I'll call all the time, you'll see. It'll be fine,' I say, and I wonder who I'm trying to make feel better, Mama or me? Mama looks at my face like she's trying to memorize me, and I want to tell her the truth: that I will miss her more than the whole wide world and the stars and the moon all mashed up together. But I can't. I can't hardly even think about it without my eyes starting to burn and that big, ugly lump growing in my throat and cutting off all my words.

I hear the Ryders' car before I see it, rumbling down our little oak lane, dipping and bobbing across the dirt road, and kicking up a storm of dry red dust. I bet it's never been on a dirt road in its life. Mama stands up and waves. I can feel my heart tap dancing along my ribs, because now it is happening for real. I am actually on my way to New York City.

The car stops and the doors open. Mr and Mrs Ryder get out of the front. Mr Ryder is tall and flabby, and his collar is too tight. His face is red and sweaty from the hot car.

Miss Priss gets out of the car, too, but she stays behind the door on the other side of the car. She's wearing a new yellow dress that makes her skin look sick and green.

'Hi, Casey, dear,' Mrs Ryder says, and I smile because I like Mrs Ryder, even if she is Miss Priss's mom. Mr Ryder doesn't say anything, just wipes his forehead with his handkerchief and gets back into the car. I pick up my suitcase with one hand and use my leg to shift it down the steps, dragging it through the dirt to the back of the car while Mama talks to Mrs Ryder. My palms are red and slippery.

'Thank you so much for taking Casey with you,' I hear Mama say, but my heart is pounding too hard to hear anything else. The air is hot, but inside I am cold as ice. I am leaving Warren and Mama, and going to dance in New York City. I am excited and scared and jittering all over.

The trunk of the car opens and Miss Priss is standing next to me. She looks at me like she wants to say something, but I don't give her a chance. I just put my suitcase in the back and turn away. I don't have time for Miss Priss and her comments today.

I give my mama one last hug. I want to tell her that I am going to miss her, but I can't make the words come out past the lump in my throat, so instead I just press my head into her shoulder and try to breathe her in so deep I'll never forget her smell. Mama squeezes me back hard and then steps back holding onto my shoulders and looking in my face.

'You work hard, Casey Quinn.' She nods her head once, then steps back while I climb into the car.

The hot leather seat burns the back of my legs. Mr Ryder starts the engine before I even close the door and I don't manage to shut it until halfway down the dirt lane as we're bumping toward the main road. I turn around in my seat and look out the back window, waving at my mama until we are out of Warren.

The car ride is shorter than the bus ride, because we don't stop at every town to pick people up and let people off. Mr Ryder drives fast, blowing his horn at anything that slows him down. The white dotted line at the side of the road blurs together, and the wind whips in through the open car windows. Miss Priss keeps stealing sideways looks at me, but I pay her no mind. I rest my head on the side of the car and let the warm breeze wash over my face.

The sun rises higher and higher in the sky, but Mr Ryder doesn't slow down. I can feel my stomach start to rumble. We're in Maryland now and I wish Mama had packed me some sandwiches.

'Dear,' Mrs Ryder says, 'aren't we going to stop for lunch?'

Mr Ryder doesn't answer, but we stop at the next roadside diner. The air feels cool and fresh compared to the hot car, and I stretch my arms up into the sky and try to shake some feeling back into my toes.

There's a flashing blue neon light that says *Eats* in the window, and the waitresses wear blue dresses with frilly white aprons and badges with their names on. A waitress named Shirley takes us to our table.

'Well, I'm starving. What are you going to have, Casey?' Mrs Ryder asks me as we slide into our booth, the vinyl squeaking against my legs.

I have a hamburger, so does Mrs Ryder and after Mr Ryder orders a cheeseburger, Ann-Lee does, too.

'I hope you're gonna watch your weight when you're living on your own,' he says to her. 'I didn't pay good money on ballet school for you to throw it away by packing on the pounds.'

Miss Priss picks the cheese off her burger before she eats it.

After lunch Miss Priss and I wait outside while Mrs Ryder pays for lunch and Mr Ryder fills up the tank with gas. I can feel her eyes on my face like they are needles digging into my skin, but when I turn to look at her, she looks away.

'What?' I ask, making my voice hard as rock because I am tired of her snakey eyes staring at me.

'Aren't you scared?' she asks in a voice so small I almost don't hear it.

My heart drums hard against my ribs and my palms go cold, but I don't say anything. Of course I am scared, just a little, but I'm not gonna let anyone know it. Especially not

Miss Priss. She'd probably lap up my fear like a cat with cream.

Miss Priss keeps looking at me, twisting her fingers about each other and waiting for an answer.

I stand up straight and gaze back at her, level steady. 'No,' I say. 'I'm not scared at all.' And I don't say another word until we get to New York.

It is late when Mr Ryder stops the car. 'This is it,' he says. His voice is hot and tired just like the rest of us.

I hop out of the car on the double and get my suitcase out of the back. Miss Priss is staying next to her mama, holding her hand and looking up at the building in front of us like it is full of ghosts. Mr Ryder doesn't pay any attention to her nerves, though. He is straight up the steps and knocking on the front door. 'Come on,' he says. 'It's a long drive back.'

Mrs Everton's Boarding House for Young Ladies is five skinny storeys high and is made of red-brown brick that makes me think of South Carolina dirt. I miss Mama fierce in the dark, but I take a deep breath and keep my eyes dry.

Inside, the building is full of girls. Some are my age, but most are older, with their hair done up in neat curls. Their high-heeled shoes clatter against the bare boards. Upstairs someone is singing scales, and someone else is yelling at her to be quiet.

'Hello there, you must be the girls from South Carolina. I'm Mrs Everton. I've got you both in a nice room up on the second floor.'

My suitcase bumps against my leg as I heave it upstairs. Miss Priss and Mrs Ryder each have one handle of her enormous trunk, and they are carrying it up together. Mr Ryder is walking behind us, his hands jingling coins in his pocket. Our room is small, even smaller than my room back home in Warren, and it seems crammed full with two beds and two dressers squeezed in side by side.

Miss Priss takes the bed by the window.

'We'll call you in a few days to see how you're settling in,' Mrs Ryder says. 'Work hard and be good.'

She gives Miss Priss a hug and it makes me think of Mama. Missing her stings me all over, but I don't let it show.

Mr Ryder just stands in the doorway, looking at his watch.

Miss Priss looks at him with big eyes, but all he says is for her to watch what she eats and he'll have a special present for her when she comes home for Thanksgiving. She smiles, but it isn't a real smile at all.

Mrs Ryder gives her one more quick hug, and then she and her husband are gone.

Miss Priss looks lost, standing next to her bed and staring at the door.

'Well, aren't you gonna unpack?' I say, opening my suitcase on the bed and pulling out my bundle of folded belongings.

'I guess,' she says, quiet and slow.

It only takes me three minutes to empty my suitcase and put everything away in the dresser at the end of my bed. I look over at Miss Priss, but she's only managed to unpack one dress. She looks at me all hopeful. I heave a heavy sigh and start to help her. I hang up the dresses and let Miss Priss deal with her own underwear, because there is no way I am touching those.

'Thank you,' she says quietly, and sits down on the bed.

I want to shake her by the shoulders and give her face a slap. *We did it*, I want to yell. *We are here in New York City. Stop acting so humdrum, and smile.*

Instead I just sigh. 'Come on,' I say. 'Let's go find the bathroom.'

The bathroom is at the end of the hall.

'We have to share?' Miss Priss looks like she's found a bug in her breakfast.

'Of course we have to share, it's a boarding house,' I say, but she looks so lost I let her come in and brush her teeth with me. I can see her staring at me in the mirror, and it makes me uneasy. Back in Warren, I knew what was what. Miss Priss was the meanest, no-good rat-fink in the

- 159 -

town, stuck-up and spoiled as month-old whipped cream. But in New York City, she is wobbly as Gran's jello.

I spit hard in the sink and rinse out my mouth. It isn't fair. Miss Priss has been nothing but mean to me, and now she wants me to make her feel all better. I refuse. I stalk down the hall and into our room, and put on my jim-jams without a word. I can feel Miss Priss behind me, wanting to talk, wanting to be my best friend. Miss Priss can go jump in a lake. I pull the covers over my head so just my eyes peep out, and stare out the window.

'Goodnight?' Miss Priss says.

I don't say anything, and the bedroom light goes out with a click.

Outside the street is full of life. I can hear the cars driving past, and their headlights flick up through the window and move across our wall. There's another sound, too, a sort of low snuffling coming from Miss Priss's bed. I know without listening too hard that she is crying. It makes me feel a little sorry for her, but I don't want to feel sorry. Not for Miss Priss. Not for anyone. I close my ears to the crying and listen to the sounds of the City.

Chapter Twenty-Two

I wake up early and for a minute I don't know where I am. The sound of footsteps outside my door, and cars rushing past on the street make me sit up bolt straight. And then I remember. I am here. I am in New York City. I smile wide as wide can be and sit up, as awake as my smile.

Miss Priss is snoring in the next bed. How can anyone sleep on a day like this? I get dressed quietly, dancing from foot to foot and trying not to let the floorboards creak under my feet. There is a deep well of worry in my stomach, because today is the first day of high school, but I swallow it away. I am Casey Quinn, and nothing is gonna stop me now. Besides, in her last letter Andrea promised to meet me near the school so we could walk in together. I wonder what it will be like to go to school and have someone to sit with. Just thinking about it makes me smile even more.

Downstairs, the kitchen is full of elbows and legs pushing to get to the stove where there is a big pot of porridge bubbling. It is still too warm for porridge, and my stomach isn't in the mood for food. I see Miss Priss's feet on the wooden stairs and I scoot out the front door. I am not walking to my first day of new school behind Her Majesty. No way. I close Mrs Everton's front door behind me. Then I take a deep breath and start walking.

I walk hard and fast, keeping my eyes open for the street signs. I've practiced this walk in my head with my map a million times, but now that I am actually doing it, everything is different from how I imagined it. The streets are bigger and full of people shoving their way to work. And no one spares a second to look at me, even with my ratty-tatty high-tops slapping along the sidewalk.

Everyone looks like they know where they are going, and it makes me feel lost right away. But when I look up, I can see the street signs clear as you please and I follow them past the big brown houses on Mrs Everton's block, past the park and toward the City where the buildings are so high I can hardly see the sunshine.

I am so busy watching the signs that I don't see Andrea

until she is right in front of me.

My feet stop fast. I am breathing hard. She is standing on the other side of the street, waving at me. I wave back and my heart flip-flops in my chest, because part of me thought she wouldn't really be here. That it was too good to be true. But she is here.

The lights finally go red and the cars stop, and we run into the middle of the street.

'Casey!' Andrea shouts. Her smile is bright and wide, like a crescent moon, and her brown curls bounce around her face. 'You made it!' She wraps her arms around me, and I laugh because I don't know what else to do.

'You're here!' I say.

'Of course I'm here. I said I'd be here, didn't I?'

I nod, but I still can't believe it, not really. The lights change and a taxi blares its horn. Andrea grabs my arm, and pulls me out of the street and back onto the sidewalk.

My heart is still hammering as Andrea slips her arm through mine. We walk down the sidewalk together. It seems like the whole City is alive. Gusts of hot steam shoot out at us from the subway vents, making me jump. Andrea laughs, but she isn't laughing at me. And I laugh, too.

Andrea tells me about living with her big sister and her husband and their new baby in a tiny two-bedroom apartment, but she says it doesn't matter, because when she is a famous ballerina she will have her own penthouse and a bathroom all to herself so she can soak in the tub as long as she likes without her brother-in-law's smelly socks hanging from the shower rail.

'My sister's impossible,' Andrea says, rolling her eyes. 'And all she thinks about is the baby. I wish I could live in the boarding house with you. We'd have so much fun.'

'I wish you could, too,' I say. 'I have to share a room with Miss Priss.'

'That stuck-up girl from the audition? Don't worry, I'll give her snake-eyes at ballet lessons for you.'

Andrea grins at me, and I grin back. A bit uneasy, because I've never had a friend before, not really. I've had Mama and Gran, but they're family. This is different.

'Oh, I forgot! Show me your class schedule, the one the school sent you,' Andrea says.

I open my bag and pull out the folded piece of paper that was mailed to Mama.

Andrea holds up a piece of paper just like it and looks at them together. Then she crows.

'See, we're in the same homeroom, and in English and math together. They split us up for science, but we have the same lunch block and everything.' She smiles at me and her curls seem to bounce with joy.

'Come on, we'll be late,' she says, and pulls me faster along the sidewalk.

New York City is so different from Warren I can hardly believe it. Back home I stuck out like a sore thumb, but New York is too full of people for anyone to notice me at all. It makes me feel good, like I fit in, but it makes me feel kind of lonely, too. Like no one in the world would notice if I slipped and fell into a subway grate. It makes me real glad to be walking to school with Andrea.

As we turn a corner I see a big brick building with 'Lincoln High School' carved in stone on the front. There must be hundreds of other students streaming in through the doors. Andrea and I join them. Everyone is moving fast, shoving books and bags into lockers.

'Come on,' Andrea says. 'The first bell must've already gone.'

The halls are enormous, and there must be fifty doors to choose from. I look down at my schedule.

'Where do you think we need to go?' I ask, feeling dizzy with the smell of bleach and old shoes.

Andrea looks around. 'This way.'

We tumble through the door of our first classroom, laughing.

The whole room turns to look at us, and I choke the sound back into my mouth, but Andrea doesn't stop moving. She pulls me to the back of the room, and we sit side by side in two empty desks.

A second later the door opens again. The teacher comes in. Her name is Miss Spitz and she looks sour as a pail full of crab apples, with pointy cat's glasses on a long chain. There is a buzz and crackle as the loudspeaker turns on, and it makes me jump in my seat. Andrea puts her hand over her mouth to hide her giggle, and I can feel the laugh bubbling up inside of me, too, but one look from the front of the room and I pinch my lips together and keep quiet. 'Can you believe her glasses?' Andrea says as we head to our next class. She crosses her eyes, and I laugh. 'Right, we've got math next. I think that must be upstairs.'

The hallways are full of students, the sound of hundreds of feet and voices louder than I could ever have imagined back in Warren. This is high school, too, so everyone is older than us. I feel very small.

Math is the worst, but the class is so big, it's easy to find a seat in the back. The teacher is young and pretty, but I don't think she likes being a teacher very much. She just looks tired as she hands out our textbooks and tells us to start reading from page one.

Andrea and I get split up for science. Being split up is awful, but the science class isn't so bad. Mr Eisner is a creaky old man, but he spends the class demonstrating different-colored explosions behind a big glass plate. The room is so filled with smoke by the end of class, we can hardly breathe. I can't imagine ever getting to do an experiment in Warren.

At lunch, I am lost for a minute. The cafeteria is bigger than the whole school building back home, and it is buzzing with too many people to count. But I won't let them scare me. Besides, they hardly even notice me. I stand up straight and get in line for lunch.

'Casey, up here!' Andrea is further up the line, and I scoot in behind her.

'What is this?' I say as we sit down on the picnic bench in the playground.

'I think it's supposed to be macaroni and cheese.'

But it don't look nothing like Gran's, or Mama's. The cheese is wet and runny, and the pasta is so hard it's crunchy. I wrinkle my nose, and shudder as I eat.

Suddenly I see Miss Priss. She's eating macaroni and cheese, too, but she's sitting alone, her eyes big and red like she's been crying. For a moment, I feel sorry for her. And then I make myself remember all the times she tripped me at lunch, sitting with her ballet bunch and sneering at me 'cause I ate all alone. Serves her right, I say to myself.

'What are you looking at?' Andrea asks, turning around.

'Nothing,' I say, and I don't look in Miss Priss's direction again.

Chapter Twenty-Three

After school Andrea and I skip away quick. We're both excited about why we are really here, to dance.

'That was awful. We already have ten tons of homework and it's only the first day.' Andrea pretends to stagger under the weight of her books.

We walk together, talking about our day, until we get to the end of the street.

'Well, this is where I go left and you go right,' Andrea says.

I stop and look at my feet. They are pointing toward the dance studio, but seem stuck to the sidewalk. I look up at Andrea. My lungs are so full of words, none of them can get out.

'I'll see you tomorrow?' I ask, and it is a question.

Andrea just rolls her eyes. 'Of course, silly. Same place, same time, rain or shine! Good luck at your lessons.'

'You, too,' I say. Then my feet pull free, and I turn around and skip the other way, dancing my joy to the beat of other people's feet, and not caring one bit who looks my way.

It is only two more blocks to Miss Martha's studio. I push through the door with a flourish. I want to bow, because here I am. But the woman behind the desk doesn't even look up. I walk over to her and wait.

'Can I help you?'

'I'm Casey Quinn,' I say. 'I'm here for my lessons.'

The woman looks at me, from the top of my head to the bottom of my scruffy old high-tops.

I wait for her to sniff, or maybe even scowl. But she doesn't.

She smiles. 'Up the stairs. Changing rooms are on the right.'

As I walk up the stairs, the air is already filled with the sound of music looping through it like a crooked top. My heart jumps up, ready to join in.

In the changing room I wriggle out of my school clothes and pull on the dance outfit Gran made me. It's a good thing I made holes in my tights, because I've grown another inch this summer.

There are two other girls in the changing room. They both look shy and nervous, sitting on either end of a long bench.

'Hi,' I say, because Andrea has made me brave. 'I'm Casey.'

They look up sharpish, like startled rabbits.

'Well, I guess I'd better go in.' I think back in Warren I would have worried they didn't like me, but in New York I don't care.

I waltz my way into the dance studio, the two other girls close behind me. There is a woman at the front, stretching herself out on the floor. I recognize her from my audition. She's the one who showed us how Miss Martha wanted us to move. She is long and lithe as a willow tree bowing its branches to the river.

The room fills up with the rest of the class. They all seem nervous, too, looking about the room with wide eyes.

Then the door to the classroom opens. Miss Martha doesn't just walk into a room. She *arrives* and everyone knows it. It's like the air changes around her and we can all feel it. We stare at her. Even if I was blindfolded, I think I would know she'd arrived. She sweeps in, wearing a long-sleeved black leotard and full black skirt. With one clap of her hands, the entire room lines up.

'Welcome, class,' she says. Her voice is strong and fills up the room so we don't have no choice but to listen. 'This is Edith. She is a member of my Dance Company and she will be helping me teach the beginner class. It will be hard work and I expect you all to keep up. We will start with basic drills. First you will observe Edith.' She nods to the pianist, and he starts playing.

Edith steps to the middle of the floor and sits down. Her back is to the room, her long black hair hanging over it like a curtain, but I can see her face in the large mirrored wall in front of us. Her eyes are open, but she isn't looking at herself. She's looking somewhere far away.

The music shifts and Edith begins. First with bounces like we did at the audition, sitting with our soles together and bobbing our bodies toward our feet. I try to memorize each movement with my muscles, just so I can do it better than before. After bounces, Edith sits straight up and begins to twist, her arms out at her sides, sweeping through the air. Then she shifts again, onto her knees. I recognize this movement from my audition, too, and it makes me think of Gran, but it doesn't hurt so much this time, because I know Gran would be proud to see me here.

The music stops, and Edith returns to her original position.

'Now you will try,' Miss Martha says.

The entire class spreads itself over the floor. I am sitting right behind Edith. The music swells and away we go. I sat behind Edith so I could follow her if I needed to, but I don't. I can remember the moves like they live inside of me. Tumble. Curl. Leap. Dive. Stretch up. Higher. Up to the sky. My stomach muscles start to shake and my face is slick with sweat. But Miss Martha isn't going to let us stop now. Oh, no. We've just got started.

'Again.' Miss Martha claps. 'This time I want you to feel the movement, feel it extend out of your body and fill the room.'

The music starts again. My thighs wobble, and I grit my teeth, because I will not quit. Not on my first day, not ever. I tell my legs to stretch, and picture myself as tall as the sky, filling the room with my movements.

The music stops and so do we. Everyone looks tired, but also full of life. I look around and see one of the girls from the changing room. Her face is bright red and there's a drip of sweat hanging from her nose, but she is smiling wide. When I turn back, Miss Martha is waving us to the back of the room.

'Now Edith will demonstrate falls.'

Miss Martha barks out the counts and Edith curls slowly to the ground, coiling gracefully around her hip until she is flat on the floor, and then reverses the motions until she is standing tall and proud.

'Now the rest of you.'

My arms and legs tremble, and the muscles along the edge of my spine feel like hot flames. Miss Martha counts and I crumple in a heap on the floor. My hip crashes into the wooden floor and I wince.

'Don't hold your breath.'

I look up and Edith is standing behind me.

'Use your breath to help you.'

'Again,' Miss Martha calls.

I breathe in on the way down so that I am soft and full of air, and then out on the way up, pushing me away from the earth. Miss Martha nods and walks past without a word. I try again and again.

'Enough. Enough,' she shouts. 'This is enough for today. We will start every class with these basic drills. They are the foundation of everything I do, so I expect you to practice them. Edith will run your Wednesday class and I will see you on Friday when we will be working on moving across the floor.'

Miss Martha nods her head and sweeps out of the room. What Gran would call a Grand Exit.

I'm hot and sticky but I am happy. I sit on the floor and lean against the cool wall to catch my breath while I watch the other dancers pack up their bags and leave the room. I am breathing so hard my lungs burn like the air is on fire. Across the room, Edith smiles at me, and I blush through my already flushed skin. But I'm too tired to smile back. I close my eyes and wait for my heart to stop hammering.

As I sit there, the other dancers slowly file out of the studio.

'Bye, Casey.' The girls from the changing room are standing next to each other now, nervous. They introduce themselves as Trudy and Robin, but I don't yet have the breath to reply. Instead I smile and wave goodbye, even though my arm feels weak as a baby's.

After a while, the fire turns back into cool, fresh air and I feel strong enough to walk to the changing room. I stand up slowly, using the wall for support and wincing just a little because I am sore.

'Tough first day, huh?'

I look up sharp and see Edith standing next to me.

'Yeah,' I say. I feel shy and shabby standing next to Edith. She's wearing a beautiful green dance-dress that sings summer, and her legs and arms are full of grace.

'What's your name?'

'I'm Casey Quinn,' I say, sticking out my chin and trying not to breathe too hard.

'Well, Casey Quinn, you did really well.'

'Really?'

'Really. Even Martha was impressed.'

'She didn't say anything.' I say.

'Martha won't say if she likes you, but if you are doing something wrong, she'll let you know. Believe me.'

'Thanks,' I say.

Edith moves back into the middle of the floor and starts stretching again.

'Aren't you going home?' I ask, moving toward the studio door.

'No, I've got rehearsal with the Company in ten minutes.'

'Oh,' I say softly.

'I'll see you on Wednesday,' Edith says. 'And don't forget to stretch before you go to bed tonight, or else you are going to be sore in the morning.' And with that she disappears back inside her dancing.

The changing room is empty when I step inside, and I take a long shower, not too hot and not too cold, stretching and flexing my muscles under the water.

I dry off in double quick time and pull on my street clothes. My hair is a mess, but there isn't much I can do about that. I try to pat it back into its normal place with my fingers, but it doesn't do much good. Gran would say

I look like a ragamuffin. Next time I'll remember to bring a comb. I look hard at my face in the mirror. I wonder if I look different now that I'm dancing in New York City, if anyone could tell. But I'm still freckly old Casey Quinn, as far as I can see. I just wear a bigger smile now.

When I step back into the hallway, there is music coming from the dance studio. I know it isn't my place to pry, but I can't help myself. I push the door open a sliver and peek through.

There is Edith, dancing with the Company. Miss Martha is sitting in the director's chair in the corner of the room. Her back is to me, but I don't dare open the door any further.

I squeeze my face right close to the door and watch the dancers. They move together like the leaves on a tree being blown by a single wind, or a swarm of starlings twisting and turning through the evening sky, all making a single shape. The dancers swooping across the floor, all making a single dance. My middle feels empty with the want to join in, and I stretch and bounce along with them.

The music ends softly and I shut the door before I'm seen. I walk down the stairs slowly, light as a feather on a breeze. I am already itching for it to be Wednesday, to dance again. And now I am itching for something else, too. I step onto the City street and breathe in the rush all around me: the traffic, the chatter of feet, the flutter of pigeons cooing like they think they're doves. I am itching to dance with Miss Martha's Company.

I sway down the sidewalk, weaving in and out of the other walkers like we are all dancing together – like I know where they're gonna be before they move their feet.

Chapter Twenty-Four

I do stretch before I go to bed, but it don't make one lick of difference. I am still sore in the morning, like I've been stretched out on a taffy hook and left hanging. I can hardly hobble down the stairs. Each step feels like red-hot pokers are hitting my legs.

I shuffle slow and steady to school, not looking up from my feet for fear of tripping. I get to school as the first bell rings, and creak like a rusty hinge into my seat. Andrea isn't here and I watch the door, waiting for her to come in.

The second bell rings, still no Andrea.

We are all halfway through the Pledge of Allegiance when she opens the door. The whole room looks at her, and Miss Spitz frowns hard.

Andrea turns bright red and takes the seat next to me. I smile, but she just glares, and when the bell rings for us to change class she doesn't wait for me.

Andrea ignores me all day and by the afternoon the worry worm in my middle is writhing around, making me feel green-sick.

After school I try to wait so she'll walk out with me, but she just looks very busy with her locker and I know she won't leave until I'm gone.

The school steps are steep and I wince, taking one at a time. I can feel Andrea behind me, moving slow so she doesn't have to walk with me.

We head down the sidewalk like a pair of shadows.

'Can't you go any faster?' Andrea calls after what seems like forever.

I turn around slowly. 'No,' I say, angry and tired and sore.

We are staring at each other.

'Where were you this morning?' Andrea scowls.

Her words hit me hard, knocking the breath out of my lungs, and I can't say a thing.

'I waited for you for ages. We were going to walk to school together, remember?'

My mouth is desert-dry. 'I'm sorry. I forgot,' I say, but it doesn't make things any better.

'You *forgot?*' Andrea is giving me the stink eye now, and I can feel my heart sinking. I thought I was going to have a friend in New York.

'I'm really sorry,' I whisper again, then someone bumps into me and my legs sway like jello. The wobble hurts and I scrunch up my face with pain.

Andrea scowls again, but I can see the corners of her mouth twitching. I crunch my face harder, peeking at her through tight eyelashes. I can't believe I forgot about Andrea, and I think the truth must show on my face.

'You're a strange one, Casey Quinn,' Andrea says, rolling her eyes. 'OK. I forgive you, but don't forget again. Friends don't leave each other waiting on the street.'

She slips her arm through mine, and I wince a little.

'So was it a tough class, then?' she asks, grinning as we limp down the sidewalk.

'Everything hurts,' I say.

'Tell me about it. Our teacher made us lie on our stomachs with our legs bent like frogs, and then he stepped on our backsides to make sure our hips are flexible enough.'

'How could he tell if they aren't?' I ask.

'If your feet pop up in the air, you need to work harder,' Andrea says grimly. 'Hey, don't laugh, it isn't funny.'

'I'm sorry,' I say, 'but I can't help picturing all of your legs . . .' I can't finish talking because I am laughing too hard. Andrea laughs, too.

'Stop it. It hurts,' she says, holding her sides, but I can't help it. We have to stop walking, and lean against the nearest building to hold ourselves up.

'Hey, want to come to my house to do homework?' Andrea asks when we can breathe again.

'OK,' I say.

Andrea lives in a two-bedroom apartment on 58th Street with her sister's family. They live on the eleventh floor.

'Are you crazy?' I say as I look up the steps. 'I'll never make it.'

'Don't be silly!' Andrea says, and practically drags me behind her. I am out of breath by the sixth floor, and we have to stop on the ninth because we are so hot.

'You do this every day?' I say once my lungs start working again.

Andrea nods. 'I'm gonna have killer legs by the end of the month. I'll be able to grand jeté over the other dancers' heads!'

We giggle our way up the last three flights, and burst through the door to Andrea's apartment, still laughing.

'Shhhhhh! You'll wake the baby!' Andrea's sister hisses loudly at us from the sofa. She's holding a small bundle of white all wrapped up in a blanket. I think if anything is gonna wake a baby, it'll be the person holding it and yelling, but I don't say a word.

'Casey, this is my sister, Linda,' Andrea says, rolling her eyes. 'Linda, this is my best friend Casey Quinn.'

I smile wide. *Best friend.* The words just about make my heart glow, and my toes start to tap over the floor. Linda looks at me with squinty eyes, and I stand still. She's very beautiful, but she looks very tired, too, like she hasn't slept proper in all her life.

'It's very nice to meet you, Casey, but I just got Alice to sleep, and if you wake her up, so help me I will box your ears.'

'We'll be quiet,' I say, because Linda looks like she might be serious.

Andrea and I go to the kitchen, which is a tiny room the size of a pickup truck, crammed full with a sink, a stove, a refrigerator and a table to sit at.

'Linda's not so bad really, she's just been really grumpy since Alice was born. You want something to drink? We've got lemonade.'

Andrea pours us each a glass while I get out our books and set them on the kitchen table. Homework goes fast when we put our heads together. Andrea is good at math and helps me with the tough problems.

'So, tell me all about your first dance class,' she says.

'It was amazing,' I say. 'Really hard, but I can't wait to go back. And after class, I saw the Company practicing. They are better than amazing.' I am on my feet and dancing in the tiny square of free floor in the kitchen. Showing Andrea how they swoop and turn and twist their bodies. 'But they're all doing it together, and someday I'll dance with them, too.' The words are out of my mouth before I realize, and I stop suddenly, because I never dared tell people my dreams in Warren. But Andrea doesn't laugh, she just glows.

'I know you will, and I'll be a New York City Ballet principal, and we'll be famous dancers touring the world!' she says, curtseying low and graceful, every inch a ballerina. 'And then we'll come back and live in the penthouse at The Ritz and have our own show on Broadway!' Andrea spins in a perfect *pirouette*, but the room is too small and her hand knocks the back of a frying pan, sending it clattering across the kitchen floor.

'SHHHHH!' Linda hisses at us from the other room, and we cover our mouths to quiet our giggles.

'I should go. I need to be back at Mrs Everton's.'

'OK,' Andrea whispers. 'I'll see you tomorrow. Don't forget to practice. I don't want to get to The Ritz before you!'

I nod hard. I will practice. I'll dance until I turn blue, and then I'll keep right on going.

After school on Wednesday, I can't wait to get to Miss Martha's studio. I have been practicing basic drills in my room at night when Miss Priss is out, and I can feel them running through my veins.

I am into my dance clothes and in the studio quick as a flash. I start warming up right away. Every bounce still hurts, but the more I move, the more I can feel my muscles loosen. Trudy and Robin warm up with me, and slowly the other students come in and join us. It feels good, to dance with other people and not just by myself. I shift positions and the room seems to shift with me. I count ten bounces with my feet together, and then I spread them wide, trying to do it like we've been taught. I count ten bounces and change again, and everyone else changes, too.

Edith comes in at four o'clock sharp, just as we all change positions again. She stares at me and I can feel heat rising to my face, but I keep going. Then she claps her hands just like Miss Martha.

'OK, we'll start with basic drills, just like on Monday. Do you all remember them?'

I nod my head proudly. I could remember basic drills in my sleep. But not everyone looks so sure.

'It's OK if you don't remember everything. It's only

your second class,' Edith says. Then she looks at me. 'Casey, maybe you can demonstrate.'

My face flushes radish red as I walk to the middle of the room where Edith is pointing for me to stand, but when the music starts I forget all my worries and I just move.

'Good,' Edith says. 'Now all together. Casey, stay where you are.'

We go through the exercises again, Edith walking around us and correcting small mistakes, reminding everyone to keep breathing.

After dance class, I am weak and wobbly as a kitten. But I am smiling.

'Hey, Casey, would you show me how you do your falls?' a boy with short blond hair asks. His name is Kevin.

I am not used to people talking to me, and asking me for help. In Warren no one hardly gave me the time of day.

'OK,' I say. 'Will you count it for me?' I feel shy, but I take a deep breath and listen to Kevin's counts, coiling my body into a spiral until I am flat on the ground. Then I reverse the move, growing like a bean sprout winding its way toward the sun.

I count for Kevin while he tries the fall. He rests too heavily on each beat, freezing in place instead of contracting in one smooth motion, but I don't say anything. I just smile.

'Thanks,' Kevin says. The other students have left now, and I can see Edith watching us as she warms up for her rehearsal with the Company. 'I think it makes more sense now. I'll see you Friday!'

I wave as he walks out the door.

'Casey,' Edith says, 'can I see you before you leave?'

My heart leaps up into my mouth and I swallow hard to get it back into place. 'I'm sorry,' I say fast as the words can come off my tongue, because it isn't my place to teach at all. I'm just a beginner, and Edith must think I am way too big for my britches showing Kevin how to do a fall when I only just learned it myself.

'Don't be silly,' Edith laughs. 'We all help each other. That's how we learn. I just wanted to ask if you had a few minutes. I want to teach a new floor sequence next week and it would be great if you could help me demonstrate again. That way I can really look at how everyone is doing instead of trying to see them in the mirror.'

'Me?' I say, 'cause it is too good to be true.

'Yes, you. You're a quick learner, and I can tell you're dedicated.'

I nod hard. There is no one more dedicated to dance in the whole wide world.

'So will you be my assistant?'

'Yes!' I just about shout it, and Edith laughs. Her laugh is gentle and kind like water rippling down a brook, and it makes me like her even more than I did before.

'OK. If you can stay an extra twenty minutes or so after class, I can teach you the routines, and then the next week you'll be my demonstrator.'

So on Wednesdays, I stay late after class and Edith teaches me something new before she starts rehearsals with the Company. Sometimes, when Miss Martha is away, she even lets me stay for the Company rehearsal, and I sit quiet as I can manage in the corner of the studio, soaking up their movements and dreaming about the day I'll be dancing with them.

Chapter Twenty-Five

It is November, and there is snow everywhere. New York City is cold. And I don't mean cold like a little shiver or a shake. I mean cold like you're freezing all the way down to your bones and five days in front of the fire wouldn't warm you up.

I walk along the sidewalk, clutching my coat close. The wind is hollering at me and trying to push me back, but I am on my way to Thanksgiving dinner with Andrea and her family, and nothing would turn my toes around. I see Andrea waiting on me up at the next corner and I put some more pep into my steps, stomping through the slush in my high-tops like it's nothing but dry dust.

'Hi, Casey,' she says, her breath making perfect round puffs of steam with every word. 'Are you sure you want to do this? It's crazy in there! Alice won't stop bawling and I think Linda's gonna explode. We could just go hide in Central Park or something.'

'It'll be great,' I say. And I want it to be true. It's my first Thanksgiving away from home, without Mama and Gran, and it hurts every time I think about it. I try to smile but the air makes my teeth feel brittle, like shards of ice, and I close my lips tight. 'Come on, let's get inside!'

Andrea laughs and puts her arm around my shoulder. She says I feel the cold more on account of my thin south-ern blood, but I can see she feels it, too. Her shoulders are all hunched up like a tawny owl.

We hurry along the sidewalk, weaving in and out of the other people, their heads down and bundled up against the frost. We stick close to the building side of the sidewalk. I learned the hard way what it feels like to be splashed by street slush when a yellow-checkered cab drives by.

The wind digs its fingers through the thin spots in my coat and makes my freckles stand on end. I may be on a scholarship, but I still need to pay Mrs Everton room and board. Mama sends me money once a month. It's enough for rent, but not for extras, and it certainly ain't enough for a brand-new coat with rabbit-fur lining like the one Miss Priss says she's gonna bring back from home after Thanksgiving.

Still, I don't let Miss Priss bother me anymore. I've got Andrea and Edith. And who does Miss Priss have? No one. Not even the ballet girls at Mrs Everton's like her much. I guess new shoes don't count for a lot in New York. I can hear Mama inside my head telling me to be more kind, and Gran saying I should be more Christian, but I don't want to listen.

Andrea and I bustle through the door of her apartment building. The warm air hits me real hard. My nose starts to run, and my fingers and toes quiver and itch like a mountain of fire ants. And by the time we climb up eleven flights of stairs I am so hot I could drop on the spot.

'Get ready for trouble,' Andrea says, opening the door to the apartment.

It is a mess. Baby clothes and toys are spread all over the living room, and I can hear a wailing sound that must be coming from Alice, or maybe from Linda.

I shut my eyes and sniff the air, but there aren't any Thanksgiving smells there. No turkey, or gravy, and certainly none of Gran's candied yams full of cinnamon and spice. Part of me is glad there aren't any good smells, because good food would make me think of Mama and Gran even more. And how can I enjoy a big turkey dinner and all the trimmings without them?

Andrea shuts the door softly behind us. But not softly enough.

Linda comes rushing out of the back room. Alice is squirming in her hands, hollering so loud it hurts my ears, her face almost purple as an eggplant.

'Where have you been?' she asks Andrea.

'I just went down to get Casey.'

Linda looks at me like she hadn't noticed I was here before.

'Mom and Dad will be here in four hours and I haven't even put the turkey in yet.' She looks around wildly. 'David has gone to watch the football game at a bar and is picking up his parents soon. So you,' she points at Andrea, 'need to help me in the kitchen.' She turns to me. 'You hold Alice,' she says, and plunks the screaming baby into my arms and disappears into the kitchen.

Alice kicks and bucks and is much stronger than something that small should be. My ears sting with her screaming, and I worry something horrible about dropping her.

'She is so stressed.' Andrea rolls her eyes at me and sighs. 'This is the first Thanksgiving she's had to cook.'

'Is she a good cook?'

Andrea shakes her head. 'Don't say I didn't warn you.'

Alice kicks and howls again. I wrinkle my nose,

because she doesn't smell very nice, either.

'Oh, I'll change her,' Andrea says, taking the baby out of my hands and disappearing back into the bedroom.

I wipe my hands on the front of my skirt and slouch into the kitchen. Linda is sitting at the table, reading a big white cookbook and looking very confused. She glances up sharp when she hears my footfall on the linoleum.

'Where's Alice?'

'Andrea went to change her,' I say. There are bowls of half-peeled vegetables all over the counter and the biggest turkey I've ever seen in an aluminum tray on the table. Linda looks like she's going to cry.

'I don't know why I said I'd do Thanksgiving. I thought it would be easier than trying to travel with a baby, but I was wrong.'

I open the fridge and look inside. Everything you could ever want for Thanksgiving is stuffed inside.

'I can cook,' I say. I don't know why I say it, but I do.

Linda sniffs. 'Well, I can cook, but it's Thanksgiving dinner.'

'I've cooked Thanksgiving dinner before. I always helped my gran in the kitchen.' I stop then because it suddenly feels like there's a whole stuffed turkey sat on my chest. I breathe out slowly and look up at Linda. 'Let me do it. Andrea will help, and you can look after Alice and get the rest of the house ready.'

Linda's eyes are hopeful, and I can tell she wants to believe me.

'Really, I can do it. Just tell Andrea she needs to help me.' I am rinsing my hands and then rolling up my sleeves like I mean business. I start peeling the sweet potatoes just to show her that I can.

Linda drifts quietly out of the kitchen, and a moment later Andrea comes in.

'We're cooking?' she says, her eyebrows raised way up high.

'Yep,' I say. 'Put on an apron and start peeling.'

'Yes, ma'am!' Andrea salutes like a soldier, but she's smiling.

I set to work on the turkey. Gran always said the secret to the perfect Thanksgiving turkey is in the stuffing. So I stuff it full of everything delicious I can find: chestnuts, cranberries, lots of herbs and spices, and breadcrumbs to hold it all together. It makes me feel good. Like Gran is with me, showing me what to do, but it also makes me miss her and miss Mama, and it hurts to think that Mama is all alone in Warren without me.

'Wow, you really do know what you're doing,' Andrea says.

'My gran was the best cook in the world,' I say. The

words seem to stick in my throat and I swallow hard. I can feel the tears building up behind my eyes.

'Are you OK?' Andrea asks.

I nod and wipe my eyes, but they won't stay dry.

'You don't have to keep cooking if it makes you so sad,' Andrea says.

'No, it's fine.' I say, and it is. Gran loved to cook because her food made people happy. And she taught me how to cook so I could make people happy, too. I rub some butter on the turkey skin and sprinkle it with salt, then I put it in the oven and shut the door.

'It'll be the best turkey ever,' I say, and for some reason we both start laughing.

Then it's on to the vegetables while the turkey cooks. Linda sticks her head in to see if we are really working, but when I show her the turkey going golden-brown in the oven she hugs me close. Then Alice wails again, and she disappears back into the living room.

Andrea sits at the kitchen table, snapping off the hard ends of the green beans while I stir the gravy on the stove.

'So are you gonna ask her?' Andrea suddenly says.

My stomach flip-flops and my stirring hand stops. Miss Martha and the Company are giving a Winter Recital, and Edith says I should ask Miss Martha to be an understudy.

'What if she says no?' I whisper.

'So she says no,' Andrea says. 'You have to ask! What if you'd never auditioned in the first place?'

My heart hammers hard every time I even think of asking Miss Martha about dancing with the Company. I can see her raise her eyebrows and scowl down at me. Andrea snaps the last bean and brings them over to me to put on the stove.

'Come on, Casey. Look, I'm auditioning to be in *The Nutcracker* on Monday and that's terrifying, too. Be brave!'

I take a breath. Edith says I'm good. And Edith is the best dancer in the whole Company. She's performed with Miss Martha all over the world. She's been to Paris and London. I may have made it to New York City, but Edith has been everywhere. And if she says I can dance with the Company, I know I can do it.

'OK,' I say. 'I'll ask.'

And Andrea squeals and hugs me, almost tipping over my gravy pan.

At ten to three Andrea's parents arrive. We are still cooking, but Andrea pulls me into the living room. One look at her mother and father, and she leaps over the coffee table and into their arms.

It stings my eyes to look at them.

After a moment, she stands up straight and wipes her own eyes dry.

'This is Casey,' she says to her parents, waving me over to say hello.

Andrea's mother is dressed up and looking lovely, and I look down at my clothes covered in cooking spills and feel more than a little shabby, but Andrea's parents don't seem to mind.

'So you're Casey. Andrea has told us so much about you. We are very glad she has found such a good friend in the City.'

I blush to the tips of my ears, but Andrea just drags me to her room to tidy up while her parents play with Alice.

'I swear the baby always stops crying as soon as they get here. They think she's perfect,' Andrea whispers. 'Little do they know . . .'

Linda's husband David comes home with his parents at three o'clock, and we are all sitting around the table in the living room by three-thirty. The turkey sits in the middle of the table, looking as perfect as can be, and I am all aglow with pride.

Andrea's mother asks us all to bow our heads, and says grace. Then she asks us all to say one thing we are grateful for. Linda says she's grateful to be with her family, David says he's grateful for his beautiful wife and baby, and the grandparents are all grateful for Alice. Andrea says she's grateful she got into ballet school and that she's grateful she met me.

It is my turn and I am not sure what to say. I am grateful for so many things: for getting into Miss Martha's school, and Andrea, and Mama and Gran. I'm grateful for New York City and having a family to eat Thanksgiving dinner with. But it is too much to put into words, and so I smile wide and tell them all, 'I am grateful I didn't mess up the turkey.'

David says Amen, and everyone laughs. But I think they understand what I really mean.

Chapter Twenty-Six

On Monday, I can hardly sit still waiting for school to be over so I can ask Miss Martha about being an understudy for the Company. I will ask her after class, so I need to make sure I am extra-good today. The last seconds of the day seem to take hours, but when the final bell rings I am out of my chair like a leaf on a breeze.

'Wait up, Casey,' Andrea calls, and I slow down ever so slightly. We throw on our coats, scarves, hats and mittens. My back muscles clench up just thinking about the cold outside.

The air is like a frozen punch in the gut. It makes my eyes water, and little icicles form on my lashes. Andrea and I scuttle along the sidewalk, bending our heads against the wind.

'So are you going to do it, then?' Andrea asks, like she is daring me to be brave.

I nod. 'I'll ask after class.'

'You better!'

Andrea has gone all graceful since she started training at The School of American Ballet. I watch the turn of her feet on the sidewalk; she's placing them onto the slush like she's waltzing on water. She wears her hair in a bun now, too, but there are always curls escaping and they make a perfect halo around her face.

I wonder what I look like next to her. Back in Warren I was just awkward Casey Quinn, with knobby knees and high-tops that were two sizes too big. But they aren't too big anymore. I look down at my feet. My high-tops fit me just right – like I fit New York.

At the next corner, Andrea stops.

'Well, good luck,' she says and stands still, waiting.

I feel unsteady, like I've forgotten something. But my feet are already tapping to get to class, and I need to keep moving or I'll never be brave enough to talk to Miss Martha. So I skip off down the street, waving over my shoulder as I go.

I fall gratefully through the door of the school, stomping my feet and clapping my hands like a one-man band to get the feeling back into them.

In the changing room I wriggle out of my clothes. I've already got my dance outfit on underneath – another layer to keep me warm. It is warm enough inside the studio, but I am bone-cold, like a turkey in the freezer, and it will take some time to thaw out. I shiver and shudder and shake my way into the studio. Edith is there at the front, warming up as usual. She smiles at me as I take my place in the back of the class and begin my own warm-up.

Miss Martha comes into the room and claps her hands without waiting for a second. We line up on the floor, ready.

'Basic drills,' she says. Her voice is sharp and I can tell it's going to be a hard class. The music swells and we're moving. I breathe with the sound, filling my limbs up full and letting them float on the sound of the piano.

'Now, let's move across the floor!' Miss Martha claps her hands.

One two three Leap. One two three Leap!

'Come on, Casey, don't be lazy. Jump!'

I suck in my breath and try harder, even though my legs don't have much jump left in them. We go around the room two more times, and then Miss Martha claps for us to stop.

'Enough. Enough,' she shouts. She is not happy with us.

I'm hot and sticky and gasping for breath, but her

voice makes my soul cold.

'I thought you were dancers,' she says. 'Not a herd of cows.'

Everyone hangs their heads, but Miss Martha doesn't stop.

'How many times have I told you? You must think about everything you do. Every breath should be a part of the dance. Come back tomorrow. And come back dancers!'

And with that Miss Martha storms out of the room, slamming the door behind her.

There is still half an hour left of class, so Edith takes us through the exercises again, but the room feels empty without Miss Martha watching us. I stretch and kick, but I can't get loose of the feeling that Miss Martha is disappointed in me. And I know I can't ask her about being an understudy in the Winter Recital now.

When the clock hits five we stop. I lean against the cool wall to catch my breath. Edith smiles and waves as she leaves the room, but I don't feel much like smiling. I pull my clothes back on over my tights and leotard. I'm too warm, but I know I'll be freezing again once I go outside. I bundle up tight and drag-shuffle-step out of the room, down the long, dark stairs toward the door.

I am halfway down the stairs when Miss Martha's voice stops me.

'Casey Quinn, in my office, please.'

She says it like an order and I move double-quick to obey. Heart all a flitter-flutter with fear. I trip up the steps and through the red-painted door into Miss Martha's office. I know she is not happy, not one bit, and I feel weak with worry that she might send me back to Warren.

Miss Martha's office is full of pictures of her dancing. In every one she looks like she might leap off the wall and into the room. Miss Martha sits in the middle of it all, glaring at me, her face white as New York snow.

I take a big breath and hold my chin up high. I made it this far and I am not going back for no one.

'Yes, ma'am?' I say, and it is a question.

'Edith thinks you're good enough to be her understudy for the Winter Recital,' she says, raising an artful eyebrow.

My heart pounds so loud it fills up the whole room, but I can't say a word.

'What do you think? *Are* you ready?' She looks at me hard, and I stand up straight to show her that I am Casey Quinn and every inch of me is ready.

'Yes,' I say, almost leaping with the word. 'I can do it, I know I can.'

Miss Martha nods slowly.

'Well,' she says. 'We shall see.'

Miss Martha tells me to be at the Imperial Theater in

the morning for rehearsal, and waves me away. I float down the stairs on excitement. The cold barely touches my skin as I skip down the sidewalk around all the hunched-up, bunched-up souls hurrying home. I have dance to keep myself warm.

The sky is dark and New York City shines twice as bright because of it. The yellow headlights and red tail-lights twinkle like a lake-reflection under the rows of Christmas lights stretching from street to street. A clock overhead chimes six times, and I need to hurry to get back to Mrs Everton's for supper. I double-time my steps, sweeping over the stones like a skater on ice.

Chapter Twenty-Seven

The air inside Mrs Everton's Boarding House is ever-so-slightly warmer than it is outside. I wrinkle my nose. It smells like boiled cabbage. The food in New York can't hold a candle to what Mama can cook, and it doesn't even dare stand in the shadow of Gran.

I want to call Andrea and tell her the news, and then write it all down in a long letter to Mama. Mrs Everton has one phone in the downstairs hall by the bottom of the stairs. She keeps a long black book next to it and anyone who makes a call has to write it down in the book so she can charge it back. *I'm not running a charity, you know,* Mrs Everton says. *This is a respectable house for respectable ladies who pay all of their own bills.* Gran would have called Mrs Everton a Tartar, but she's all right as long as you stay two steps on her good side.

I hang up my coat in the hallway and hurry inside. But when I get to the stairs, Miss Priss Ann-Lee, who doesn't need to count her pennies, is already on the phone. She's leaning against the wall, all twisted up in the phone-cord like she means to stay there.

Her face shifts down into a scowl when she sees me tapping my toe at her, and she turns her back on me, winding another loop of phone-cord around her back. She's wearing bright pink lipstick, and I hope as hard as I can that Mrs Everton comes by and makes her scrub her face with carbolic soap. Mrs Everton's Boarding House for Young Ladies is for respectable girls, not hussies with painted lips.

I cross my arms and sit down on the bottom step. Miss Priss is giving me a this is a private conversation look over her shoulder, but I don't care. I am almost at bursting point, and I need to tell someone my news, and Miss Priss ain't gonna stop me. I lean my head against the banister and wait.

I don't mean to eavesdrop, Mama and Gran raised me better than that, but Miss Priss is talking so loud I can't help hearing.

'You promise you'll come? And we'll have Christmas in New York and stay at The Ritz?'

I roll my eyes. I bet The Ritz can't make gravy like my

mama. And there it is again, something twitching at the back of my brain, like a sour crab apple in amongst the sweet ones. Why is Miss Priss staying in New York for Christmas?

I twist the shadow thought about for a bit, trying to make it take shape, but the closer it gets the less I want to look at it, and I push it away as hard as I can.

After an eternity, Miss Priss hangs up the phone.

'Finally,' I say.

She tosses her blonde hair at me.

'I wasn't on it that long, Casey. Give me a break,' she sniffles, and I glare at her, because who is she to talk to me like that? We're both here, aren't we? She might dress all fancy but she's a South Carolina girl, just like me.

'Why are you staying for Christmas?' I ask.

'What? You were listening in?'

'Well, you talk louder than a water buffalo. It's not my fault I heard you.'

Miss Priss seems to breathe steam. 'I'm staying because I'm going to be dancing Clara in *The Nutcracker*. It's the main role.' She sniffs at me like I'm just a smear on the street. 'The ballet runs until January, so my mother and father are going to come see me perform, and we'll have Christmas at The Ritz.' She crosses her arms like it's a challenge. Other girls from the boarding house are standing on the stairs now, coming down for dinner, and they are watching us. I can feel their beady eyes on my back. But I don't care.

I forgot about the ballet auditions. I forgot to wish Andrea good luck.

My heart feels low, like a snake slithering in the grass, and there's something else, too, something even worse. But I don't want to think about it. I just want to be angry, so I stamp my feet down – *one two* – and cross my arms.

'Well, I'm performing at the Imperial Theater in Martha Graham's Winter Recital.' The words come out of my mouth before I can stop them. I stick out my chin and bite down hard, daring Miss Priss to call me a liar, even though deep down I know I am one. Miss Priss just raises an eyebrow like she doesn't believe me. And that makes me even madder.

'So you're staying for Christmas, too?' she says, and all the air comes out of me like a balloon let loose. 'Will you be staying at The Ritz?'

She bites her lip like she's sorry she said it, but I don't care. I wish I could shrivel up and shrink through the floorboards, or disappear into dust and never be seen again. I forgot about Andrea, and I didn't even think about Christmas. Christmas all alone without my mama. And I'm telling tales to impress Miss Priss, and the shame of it makes my ears burn hot as flames.

Mrs Everton rings the dinner bell and everyone moves out of the hallway. But I don't think I can face dinner. I stare at Miss Priss and she finally gets out of my way with one last sniff, but she doesn't say anything so I know I must look terrible.

I was going to call Andrea, but when I think about how mad she must be that I forgot about her audition I can't do it. Instead I dial the operator and ask to put through a person-to-person call to Warren, South Carolina. My voice trembles, and I fight to keep it firm.

'Casey?'

Mama's voice hits me first, and the missing her hits me second. It comes so hard and strong that I have to sit down on the stairs to stop from crying.

'Casey, it's so good to hear your voice. How is the City in winter? Are you keeping warm?'

Mama's voice sounds so far away down the line I can hardly speak.

'I've got all of Christmas off from the hospital, so when you come home we can spend lots of time catching up. I've really missed you. The house is so empty without you clattering about.'

And without Gran to fill it up with laughter and the sound of Perry Como . . . She doesn't say it, but I know we are both thinking it, and the thought of Christmas without Mama and Gran is too much to keep inside. The thought of Christmas together was the only way I got through Thanksgiving, and now that's been taken away, too.

'Casey, what's wrong?'

And it all comes out, like a river bursting its banks in the rainy season. Miss Martha and the Company and the Imperial Theater, forgetting Andrea's audition and how mad she must be, and not coming home for Christmas. 'Maybe I shouldn't do it, Mama?' I say, because part of me wants to just go home and hide. But Mama isn't having any of that.

'Don't be ridiculous, Casey Quinn. You are in New York to dance, not give up the second you get homesick. This sounds like a good opportunity and you need to take it.'

Mama's voice is strong. And I take a deep, shuddery breath after she says goodbye. My legs feel old and weary as I walk up the steps. The cabbage smell makes my stomach lurch.

The room I share with Miss Priss is smaller than the one I have all to myself in Warren. Miss Priss's half is decorated with ballet posters, which are OK, and cut-outs from *Teen Idol* of Frankie Avalon and Fabian, which make me feel ill.

My side of the room just has two pictures: one of Miss Martha performing, her leg sweeping her skirt through the air behind her and even her face dancing. The other picture is the one Mama painted of the leafy oak tunnel leading to our house, like it is just waiting for me to come home.

I unhook the painting and curl up on my bed, hugging the picture close to my chest. I wish Gran was here, because Gran always knew what to do. She'd tell me how to make things right with Andrea. She'd shake me by the shoulders and tell me to stop acting so selfish. But she isn't here, and I miss her and I miss Mama, and the hurt of it makes me go numb.

I close my eyes and wish Mama could come to New York City like the Ryders. But my mama can't afford The Ritz. And I wish Miss Priss would just disappear. It isn't fair that she gets everything she wants. It isn't hard for her at all.

Part of me knows that this isn't true. I'd rather miss my mama than be stuck with Mr Ryder for a pa. But it is easier to be mad than it is to be sad, so I lie on my bed and growl at Miss Priss as hard as I can.

The City feels very big, or maybe it's just that I feel so small. I keep my eyes shut, hugging my mama's painting until I fall asleep.

Chapter Twenty-Eight

wake up in the morning when it is still dark outside, but I can see the snow falling under the streetlight through our tiny window. I pad out of bed with the covers pulled tight around my shoulders, and tiptoe to the window.

My breath makes a pool of fog on the glass, and I wipe it away and peer at the snow-covered city. Miss Priss is snoring like a grizzly in the bed behind me, so I pull the blanket up over my head. New York looks like something out of a storybook. It is quiet and still, like it is just for me. Sometimes I want to pinch myself to make sure it is all true. That I really live in New York City.

I sway quietly in front of the window, watching as the snowflakes flutter and fall through the frosty air. I still feel rotten inside about Andrea. The worry worm is back, burrowing in my middle and turning my soul sour. It says I should just crawl back into bed and never show my face again, but I take a deep breath and stamp it down hard. I know what Gran would tell me to do, and since Gran isn't here to tell me to do it, I tell myself

I pull on my dance clothes, another layer on top and two pairs of socks, and creep out of the room. It may be dark but it's not that early, and there is already a pot of porridge on the stove in the kitchen. I ladle some into a bowl and hold it tight, warming up my fingers. Mrs Everton makes her porridge with water, not with milk like Gran. It doesn't taste as nice and it certainly doesn't send my toes tapping under the table, but it does warm me up inside out.

I finish my porridge and put on my coat to try and trap the heat while it's still inside me. Then I take a big breath and step outside. New York is muffled with white. I crunch down the steps, making a small rhythm with the soles of my shoes as I step down the street toward where Andrea lives. I want to see her before I go to my first rehearsal, and tell her I'm sorry.

I walk slowly up the eleven flights. I'm a lot stronger than I used to be. I don't need to stop and take a break, and I am still breathing easy when I get to the top.

'Andrea,' I whisper at the door, because it is too early for social calls. I say her name again, a little louder this time. I am holding my breath in my chest, hoping she hears me. Someone stirs behind the door, and I try to cross my fingers inside my mittens. The door creaks open. I let out the air with a whoosh of relief. It is Andrea.

'What are you doing here?' She scowls at me. The worm bites hard at my heart 'cause I can see how mad she is, but I ignore it and try to be brave. Andrea is still wearing her nightgown, and her knees are knocking together with the cold draft coming up the stairs. She pulls on her coat, puts on the boots by the door, and comes into the hall. I can tell she's still sore at me from her scrunched-up shoulders. I don't blame her, though. I'd be sore, too.

'Sorry I forgot about your audition,' I say. We sit next to each other on the top step. Somewhere in the building a baby is wailing like a siren.

'I was really nervous,' she says. 'I needed you to wish me good luck.'

I hang my head low. 'I know. I felt awful all night worrying about it.'

Andrea doesn't say anything.

'Are we still friends?' I ask, my voice quiet and scared.

Andrea looks at me, her mouth turned down at the

corners and a straight, serious line down between her eyebrows.

'Well,' she says, her face lifting a little, 'at least this time you remembered *before* I yelled at you.' She puts her arm around me. I can feel the warmth all down my spine. My shoulders start to relax.

'So did you get the part?' I ask.

Andrea shrugs.

'Well, what does that mean?' Andrea must have gotten a part. I've seen her dance and she is beauty-full of grace.

Andrea smiles at me, her curls all loose and bobbing to and fro. 'I'm a snowflake,' she says.

'That's perfect for you,' I say. I remember the snowflakes falling down and spiraling back up outside my window, floating without a weight in the world. I think Andrea can see I am impressed because her smile grows even wider.

'It's not the main part. Your friend Ann-Lee got that . . .'

'We are not friends. We just share a room,' I say. I think of Miss Priss and her snake face with pink lips and her bragging about sleeping at The Ritz, and I scowl hard.

'Well, she's gonna be hard to live with now, that's for sure.'

I nod. Miss Priss thinks she is the bee's knees on a regular day. Now she'll be sure she's the dancing queen.

'So, what are you all twitching to tell me, Miss Quinn?' Andrea can read me almost as good as Gran.

'Miss Martha said I could be the understudy. It means I can't go home for Christmas, but Mama says I gotta take the opportunity.'

'That's great, Casey! Why aren't you more excited?'

I frown. 'I told Miss Priss I'm gonna perform, and when she finds out I'm just an understudy . . .' I can't find the words to say how low I'll feel, so I stop talking.

'Oh, don't let that grump get you down. How's she gonna know anyway? It's not like she'll be coming to see you dance, is it?'

'No,' I say slowly.

'So forget about it. If she asks, I'll say you stole the show.'

I nod and try to smile, but I still feel a fool all over for wanting to make myself big like that. Especially to Miss Priss. What do I care what she thinks?

'What's really getting you?' Andrea asks.

'I miss my mama,' I say. And I feel like a baby all over, but Andrea doesn't laugh. She just hugs me tighter.

'I understand,' she says. 'I miss my mom and dad, too, though I guess it helps to have Linda around, even if she spends all day talking about Alice. I think you're real brave to move to New York all by yourself. And when you're famous, you can fly down to see your mama in a private jet.'

I nod, but I still feel glum.

'Come on, cheer up,' Andrea says. 'We need to celebrate. Do you have rehearsal all day today?'

I nod again, a little more excited this time.

'Me, too.' Andrea thinks for a minute. 'But it's only a half-day rehearsal on Sunday. So we could meet in the cafe for a donut tomorrow afternoon?'

'That sounds good,' I say, smiling for real now.

'And don't worry about being in the city for Christmas. You can have Christmas with us.'

'What about your sister?' I say, and look darkly at her apartment door.

'Are you kidding? Ever since Thanksgiving she's been begging me to invite you!'

'OK,' I say. It won't be the same as being with Mama, but it'll be a lot better than being all by myself.

'OK, now get going. If Linda finds me out here she'll go crazy.'

I hug Andrea sudden and fierce, and she hugs me back. She looks at me with laughing eyes. 'I'll see you after rehearsal tomorrow.'

I nod, and with another quick squeeze I am back on the stairs, clattering down eleven flights, racing full force toward the door. I think if I had a sister, she would be just like Andrea, and I would love her wide as the sea.

I come crashing onto the street, which isn't empty at all anymore. It is filled with New York. People bundled up in wool coats and scarves walking into town to work and shop and see the sights. Their faces are all lit up with the snow, and I think there must be some magic in the fresh whiteness of it all.

I can feel the dance bubbling up inside of me. I am going to understudy for the Company. And maybe I'll even get to dance one night. The idea is almost too bright to look at.

I am one Casey Quinn and I have places to go. I step on to the curb and pass the crowds on the outside, holding my arms out wide to keep my balance.

Chapter Twenty-Nine

I get to the theater a bit before nine and stop short, staring up at the big golden door like it might open into another world. My heart beats hard. I place my hands on the large metal bar and lean against it. The door creaks open, just a small crack, and I slip in sideways. It feels like if I open the door all the way I might let the magic out.

It is cold inside and dark. My breath floats on the air in front of me. The lobby of the theater is all red velvet and gold trim like the inside of a royal jewelry box. I hold my hat tight against my head and tip my neck all the way back to stare at the chandelier hanging high up above me. Even without any lights on, it still makes my breath catch in my throat. Little flashes of sunlight split into a million rainbow dots, scattering the wall on the other side.

I hear the front door open and shut, but I don't care. I am looking up through the ceiling to the stars. It is even more beautiful than the theater I went to with Gran.

'Hi, Casey.'

I look toward the voice and see Edith staring at me. I can feel my mouth hanging open and I snap it shut. My teeth click together so sharp it hurts, and I go all red up to my ears. Edith smiles and looking at her I feel like a hill-billy.

She's wearing a soft purple swing coat and a hat she got in Paris that she calls a beret. I can see the laugh tumbling in her eyes and I stand up straight to shake off the country. But instead of laughing at me, she looks up.

'It is amazing, isn't it?' she says. 'I can't believe I forget that sometimes.'

I follow Edith through the double doors behind the lobby and step into the actual theater. It makes my jaw fall open all over again.

In front of me are rows and rows of red velvet seats that feel soft as rabbit fur against my fingers. In front of all the chairs is the stage. It has a big picture frame around it, like something from the book of fairytales Gran used to read me when I was little. Up on the ceiling, which is so high it must be miles away, is an even bigger chandelier than the one in the lobby.

I walk slowly, feet dragging on the thick carpet and up the black wooden steps leading to the stage. My legs feel oh-so-heavy, but my heart is light as a sparrow. I am standing on a real-live, honest-to-goodness New York City stage. I bow deep from my hips like President Eisenhower himself is in the audience. The sparrow in my chest is all aflutter, and my arms are fair tingling to move. I can't hardly wait for the rest of the Company to arrive so we can start dancing!

Edith is on the floor, stretching her legs like taffy. I sit down next to her.

'Thank you so much for talking to Miss Martha.' My voice is shy and soft in my throat, and I can feel my face going hot-pepper red, so I keep it pointed straight down at the floor between my knees.

'That's OK.'

Edith opens her legs to the side and lays flat on the floor between them. I can feel the stretch burn along the inside of my legs as I copy her. She holds out her hands to me and I take them. We sit toe to toe, taking turns pulling each other forward.

'Did you always want to be a dancer?' Edith asks as she pulls me.

'Yes,' I say, and then I yelp just a little as the pain shoots up my legs.

Edith laughs. 'Relax and breathe into the stretch. That's it.'

I can feel my legs letting go, like cool water running over a burn.

Suddenly the stage is full of kicking legs and reaching arms, and people rising up from the ground and falling again without a sound. The rest of the Company has arrived, and I didn't even hear them come in. I shuffle to the back of the stage, eyes wide. What if I'm not good enough at all and the whole of New York City laughs at me when I dance? Back in Warren I never gave two hoots if those know-nothing coots didn't like the way I moved, because what did they know anyway? But New York City is different.

'Hey, guys,' Edith says to the Company, dragging me forward until I'm right in the middle of them all. 'You remember Casey. She watches us rehearse sometimes. She's going to be my understudy.'

'An understudy, Edith?' one of the women says. I think her name is Helen. She glances at me with bright blue eyes. 'You must be moving up in the world. Don't tell us you're leaving?'

Then the stage goes quiet and I know Miss Martha has arrived.

She sweeps up the steps in a long black cloak and

throws it off with a flourish, dazzling us with a flash of bright green lining that Gran would call chartreuse. She is wearing her dancing clothes underneath; Miss Martha always dances with the Company. Miss Martha makes up all the dances and is always the star. Miss Martha *is* the Company.

She claps her hands. 'Places, everyone.'

The Company dancers take their positions with Miss Martha at the front. I start to step off the stage, but Miss Martha stops me.

'Casey, you will stand behind Edith and try to be her shadow. You must learn her part as if you are going to be performing it.'

My heart is drumming in my chest. I step behind Edith and swallow hard.

'Good luck,' she whispers.

Then Miss Martha nods at the piano player to begin.

The dance starts slowly at first, with just Miss Martha moving, like she is carving a space for her body in the air around her. And then, gradually, the Company begins to move behind her. Just gently at first, like the basic drills we do in class. I keep my eyes glued to Edith's back, trying to read each movement before it happens.

But as the music gets faster, I fall further and further behind. Everyone is moving in different directions and with different beats of the music, and I can't follow. They aren't anything like a swarm of starlings now. More like a swarm of bees with Miss Martha as the queen.

The music shifts suddenly and I crash into another dancer. My bones shudder.

'Casey!' Miss Martha snaps at me.

The dancers all stare. My heart sinks into my shoes when I think about Edith speaking up for me and saying I could do it. But how am I supposed to know the steps already?

'Sit down,' Miss Martha says, pointing a red talon toward the row of seats in front of the stage. I slink down the steps with a *drag-shuffle-step*, and watch as the Company dances without me. At first I am just sore. But as I watch the Company dance, the soreness sort of melts away until all I can see are Miss Martha and her dancers moving in and out of the music on stage. They run through the dance once, and then again, and I watch Edith as hard as I can, dancing along in my head with them.

After rehearsal is over, Miss Martha doesn't say anything to me. She just goes over to the piano player and starts talking about the music.

'I was terrible,' I say to Edith.

Edith puts her hand on my shoulder. 'Why don't you come early tomorrow? I'll show you the part. Just the two of us. You'll pick it up in no time.'

'Really?'

'Once you know the steps, you'll feel a lot better. OK?'

'OK!' I say.

Edith smiles and heads off to change, but I wait for Miss Martha to finish talking.

'Miss Martha?' I say quietly, because even though she is my teacher, Miss Martha still scares me just a little.

She looks at me and waits.

'I just wanted to let you know that Edith is coming in early tomorrow to help me learn the part. I promise I'll be much better at the next rehearsal.'

Miss Martha doesn't say anything. In fact, she looks almost angry.

'So Edith is going to train the perfect understudy?' she says. 'I hope she isn't planning on being sick.'

I am confused. Why would Edith do that?

But Miss Martha doesn't give me a chance to ask the question. 'Go now, I have important things to do.'

I nod, and hurry out of the theater.

Chapter Thirty

'OK, Casey, let's go through it slowly,' Edith says. 'You shadow me like last time.'

We are standing on the stage, just the two of us, and her voice echoes in the empty space.

Edith counts the beats slowly, and, as she counts, she moves. Watching Edith dance is like trying to stare at the sun, but I need to keep looking. Her arm twists out from her shoulder and I do the same, like I am sculpting the air. The beat changes and Edith falls to her knees, and I am beside her, moving from the waist to bring my head to the floor. Edith turns to look at me every few steps to make sure I am keeping up, and when she sees I am, she smiles. I follow her as we leap across the stage.

'OK, that's really good. Do you think you can do it

faster?' Edith asks. She is breathing hard and so am I.

I nod. Edith turns on the record player, and I take a deep breath and settle into my body, waiting for the music to lift me up and carry me across the stage. I can feel Edith checking on me as I move, but I keep going, letting the music tell me what to do. I kneel and leap and sway, and try to keep dancing beyond the tips of my fingers and toes. And then the silence comes and I am oh-so-still, staring across the seats to the back of the theater.

'I knew you could do it, Casey!' Edith says.

Some of the dancers from the Company are standing in the audience watching us. They clap and smile. I can feel myself going red, but Edith just grins and puts her arm around me.

'What did I tell you, guys? She's good, right?'

My smile is so wide it makes my cheeks hurt.

'Come on, let's all run it together before Martha gets here.'

The other dancers climb up on the stage and take their places.

'OK, Casey, you dance your part. I'll dance up front.'

I can see the other Company members stealing little glances at each other. But the music starts and I don't have time to think about anything but dancing.

I start from the beginning, twisting my arms slow and

strong out from my body like Edith showed me, and now I am in time with the other dancers and I can feel the beat running through all of us. Edith is dancing Miss Martha's part, curving her body around my arms and then falling away. It's like our bodies are talking to each other.

When I go onto my knees with the Company, Edith leaps up, and as the rest of us leap, she seems to fall into the floor. It is like we are two halves of a soul, pushing and pulling the space in opposite directions.

The music stops and so do we. My legs are shaky from leaping.

'Very nice, all of you.' Miss Martha's voice drifts down to us from the back of the theater. Edith steps back quickly, and the Company nod and smile, but I can tell they are nervous. Miss Martha walks silently down the aisle and onto the stage. Her eyes catch the stage lights, and sparkle in the darkened theater.

'Casey, you will observe from the audience.'

I scoot off the stage and into a seat quick. Miss Martha is talking soft, but she is in a dangerous mood. I see her glare at Edith.

The pianist arrives and takes his place at the piano.

'From the top, please,' she says, and moves into position on stage.

Miss Martha starts first, her arms sweeping through the

air around me. She is dancing the same moves as Edith, but they look so different. Miss Martha's movements are full of sorrow. I move along with the Company in my seat, twitching my muscles up and down. Miss Martha doesn't leap as high as Edith, but her face dances like it's a whole Company all by itself. I wonder what my face does when I dance. When the music comes to an end, Miss Martha steps slowly from the stage. Each step is stiff and for a second she reminds me of Gran, wobbling down the porch steps in Warren.

'Again, from the top,' Miss Martha says. She walks slowly toward me and sits by my side. Her eyes flash as she watches the dancers, studying their feet, their legs and their arms. She looks so intense I think maybe she is searching inside them to make sure they are dancing on the inside as well.

'Do you see what it is about, Casey?' she asks me.

I shake my head, and she sighs.

'It is the story of Joan of Arc, the saint, remembering the three parts of her life: Maid, Warrior and Martyr. The part you have learned is the Maid.'

I'm not sure exactly what she means, but I don't say anything.

Miss Martha waves her hand for the dancers to stop. 'Enough,' she says, 'I've seen enough. Casey, go dance

Edith's part. Edith, come sit with me.'

There is something going on. I can sense it in my stomach and I know that whatever it is is no good. The pianist begins again and we dance. Miss Martha's gaze is so heavy I can feel it, pulling me down onto the stage. My leaps are clumsy, and I grit my teeth and push harder.

'Very good,' Miss Martha says as she climbs back onto the stage when we are finished. 'Very interesting. Yes, I think this works much better, don't you?'

Edith comes back onto the stage, too. Her face is hard and angry. 'What do you mean?'

'From now on, Casey will be dancing the Maid,' Miss Martha says simply, and my stomach drops down to my toes.

There is a hum and a rustle around the circle, like a swarm of moths around a porch light. Edith steps forward, and the cold in my fingers starts creeping up my arms.

'But that's my part. Casey is my understudy,' she says, and the icy fingers snake faster.

'Oh, so you still intended to dance the Maid?'

Edith looks confused, and I want to say something to make Miss Martha stop, but I don't know how. Miss Martha keeps on talking.

'I know what you're planning. You want Casey to learn

the part of the Maid so that you can dance the part of Joan. My part.'

Miss Martha's eyes flash like they are full of fire, and Edith steps back. I realize Miss Martha is right. That's what Helen meant when she teased Edith about having an understudy. Edith didn't want me to be her understudy at all. She wanted me to dance her part so that she could take Miss Martha's.

I think Edith is going to run away, but she doesn't. She stands up straight and tall, and looks Miss Martha right in the face.

'Maybe I do want to dance the lead. I'm ready for it, and we all know you won't be able to do it for much longer.'

The room doesn't make a sound but I can feel it gasp. Miss Martha takes three steps across the circle and slaps Edith hard across the face. The slap echoes through the empty theater.

'Get out,' Miss Martha says, and we all watch as Edith gathers up her coat and slowly puts it on, still and proud, like her cheek isn't bright red from Miss Martha's hand at all.

Edith puts on her beret, and walks off the stage. At the top of the aisle she turns to face us once more, and I hope she will find the words that I can't.

But she doesn't say anything. She just stares, and when her eyes sweep across my face they could cut right through me. I feel like a leaf shriveling in a flame. I wish I could disappear into the floor. I want to call out that I didn't know, that I didn't want to take her part, but she is already gone.

'Right, that's enough for today. See you all here same time tomorrow.'

The Company dancers gather up their clothes and bags silently. I can feel them glaring at me even though they won't even look my way. They think it's all my fault. But I'm not the one who tried to take Miss Martha's part.

I put my outdoor clothes back on and I lace up my shoes slowly. I don't want the other dancers needling me with their eyes all the way down the sidewalk. When I'm sure they are gone, I walk slowly out of the theater. As the lobby door shuts I hear the music start again. I peek back through the swinging doors.

Miss Martha is on the stage dancing the role of Joan of Arc. She seems to be trying very hard to keep up with the music, and her face is so sad it looks like it might break. I close the door softly, letting it rest on my fingertips until I am sure it is fully shut, because I don't think Miss Martha would want anyone to see her that way.

*

Andrea is at the cafe when I get there. Her *pointe* shoes are around her neck and her hair is sticking out like a lion's mane. She waves me over to the counter and I climb up on one of the round spinning stools, but I don't feel much like celebrating. My head is full of Miss Martha and Edith, and there is a dread in my stomach that grows bigger with every step I take.

I order coffee and take a silent sip, as Andrea tells me about being a snowflake and flying across the stage in a flutter of feet and arms, and the insufferable Miss Priss prancing like a princess. 'We saw the pictures for our costumes today. They are all silvery, like something a princess would wear.'

The coffee is bitter and sweet at the same time, and I hold it on my tongue 'cause it makes me think of Gran.

'The dance is so pretty, and I get to be right in the front row because I'm short, so I guess it isn't so bad to be small sometimes. And there's tons of leaps, which I love. Although your friend—'

'She's *not* my friend,' I say, and Andrea giggles.

'I know, but you should see her. All she has to do is sit on a cushion at the side and watch us dance; she hardly has to move at all. But she acts like she's the prima ballerina. Mr Balanchine practically yelled at her for being a diva.'

But even that doesn't make me smile.

'What's wrong?' Andrea asks, tipping her head to one side, but I can't explain it, not even to Andrea who is so good at understanding.

'Nothing,' I say, but she knows it isn't true.

'Tell me,' she says, and I sigh heavy.

'Miss Martha gave me Edith's part.'

'Well, that's good, isn't it?'

'No, they had a huge fight and Miss Martha kicked Edith out of the show and now all the other dancers hate me.'

I feel very small. In Warren I always knew what I wanted to do, because I had a dream to be a New York City dancer. But now that I am one I don't know what to do anymore. It's so big and bright and close that it scares me, like it all might burst, or I might wake up and realize it isn't real at all. That I just dreamed the whole thing.

'Oh, they don't hate you. Besides, it's not your fault that Edith and Miss Martha had a fight, is it?'

I shake my head.

'So don't worry about it. You'll be dancing, Casey! You can show them all what you've got.'

I nod, but it's hard to look on the bright side when I've got so many tears stuck behind my eyes. I take a deep breath and let it out slowly.

'That's better,' Andrea says, then looks at the clock on the diner wall.

'I've got to run. I promised I'd be home for dinner. I'll see you on Monday, OK?'

Andrea hugs me and says she'll see me at school, and I walk back to Mrs Everton's slowly, wishing I could see Mama and wishing more than anything that I could see my gran. Gran always knew what to say, and she believed in me like nobody in the world. *You follow your dreams, Casey,* she'd say. Just remembering her say it makes me feel a tiny bit better. My steps get lighter through the snow, leading me all the way home.

Chapter Thirty-One

On Monday there are only five more days until Christmas vacation.

It is cold outside again, and the sky looks heavy with snow as I slip-slide toward class. My feet slow down. *Step. Step. Stop.* As I get close to Miss Martha's I go all weak and panicky, that evil, wriggling worm burrowing back into my belly. But I won't let it. Not this time. I'm not afraid of snakes, so that worm won't so much as dare to show its face. No little dance studio is gonna make my knees shake.

I speed up again, stepping one foot in front of the other faster and faster, until I'm rolling down the sidewalk like a steam train *one-two-three-four-one-two-three-four,* my breath coming out in little puffs of steam.

I burst through the door and up the steps without

slowing down. And then I stop dead cold. Because there is Edith warming up in the middle of the room, same as always, and definitely not looking my way.

I feel sick as sick can be and go straight to the back of the room to change, pulling off my outside clothes quiet as I can. Everything I do sounds loud, like all of a sudden I'm some clumsy elephant.

I sit down all silent on the floor and start to stretch myself out. My muscles are bunched up and protesting from the cold and the worry.

When I look up, Edith is standing in front of me. I hold my breath and get ready to fight, 'cause that part is mine now and no one is going to take it away from me. But Edith doesn't yell at me. She just sits down and offers me her hands.

I am nervous, but I put my hands in hers and we sit foot to foot, stretching back and forth on the floor until I can't keep quiet anymore. The words spill out of me like my very own snowstorm.

'I didn't know she was gonna give me your part,' I say. 'Honest I didn't. I would have said something.' I stop then, because there is nothing I can say that could ever make it any better. I stop and Edith smiles, just a small smile but it is a smile all the same.

'It's OK, Casey. It isn't your fault. I wanted you to be

there in case Martha couldn't dance. I wanted her part. It was a gamble and it blew up in my face, didn't it?'

I feel red-raw with shame, 'cause there's no way I'd be so kind if it was the other way round. I think Edith is the bravest person I know. I don't know if I'd have the guts to show my face.

'Why did you come back?' I ask, but what I really want to ask is, How? How did you get so brave?

Edith laughs at me and tugs me forward. I feel my muscles protest again.

'I'm a Graham dancer,' she says, like it's the simplest thing in the world. 'Martha would never let me back if I went and sulked, and I want to be here when she finally admits she's too old to keep dancing some of her roles.'

'Do you really think she isn't good enough?' I ask, whispering like Miss Martha might hear me. Edith shrugs and pulls me back to the floor.

My head spins. I can't imagine anyone saying Miss Martha shouldn't dance, but then I think about how tired she looked practicing up on stage.

'Some day she'll need one of us to dance for her and I plan to be around when that happens. So I'll keep coming back, no matter what she throws at me.'

Edith is quiet for a minute. 'Casey, I want you to know.

I didn't just pick you to be my understudy just so I could dance the lead. You are a good dancer and I know you will do a great job with my part.'

The door bangs open and Miss Martha sweeps in, and I go all guilty, like I was the one talking about taking her place, not Edith at all. I hold my breath because I think Miss Martha is going to shout and yell. But she doesn't. She just claps her hands for music.

After class, I walk to the Imperial Theater for rehearsal with the Company. No one is even a little impressed by how well I know my steps. They're just thinking, *That Casey Quinn is no Edith.* I grit my teeth and dance harder, curling my body across the floor like nothing can hold me back, because I will show them that I deserve to be here. That I'm a born dancer with passion and fire fair leaping out of my skin.

We dance until it is well past dark, but I keep going and don't let anyone see I am tired. My legs burn down to the bone, but I tell them to be quiet and leap, and they listen.

'Enough,' Miss Martha says, and stops sudden in the middle of the floor. In the mirror her face is white and weary. She doesn't turn to look at us, just says we've done enough for the day and waves us away. I am bone tired and I lean against the wall to keep my balance as I pull my outside clothes on top of my tights and leotard. And I hold the railing all the way down the stairs.

Back at Mrs Everton's house, I hang my coat on my hook and shuffle-step-slouch into the kitchen. My heart sinks low down in my belly because Miss Priss and some of the new ballet crew are already there, lounging over the table like they own the place.

I set my shoulders square and walk past them to the icebox, busying myself inside like I don't have time to be bothered with their ballet talk and I'm not tired at all. But they aren't talking about ballet.

My hands and heart go cold, and it's nothing to do with having my head in the icebox. Miss Priss is talking about her parents and all the things they are going to do together in New York City. Staying at The Ritz, The Rockettes at Radio City Music Hall, carriage rides in Central Park. Each word hurts like a million tiny pin-pricks, making me think of Mama and how I'm missing her terrible.

'Are you playing penguin or something?' one of the girls shouts at me, and I stand up real slow and shut the icebox door. I'm not hungry anymore.

My eyes sting, but I breathe in the crying with a deep breath because I will not cry in the kitchen in front of

Miss Priss Ann-Lee. I give her the most hateful look I can manage, and then walk out of the room like they aren't nothing more than lazy flies gathering in my way.

I am only halfway up the stairs before I can't hide the sadness anymore and the first fat teardrop hits my shoe. My feet start running, trying to race the crying back to my room.

We get there all at the same time and I sob face down into my pillow. My tears are hot and angry, because it is not fair that Miss Priss can have everything when I can't. It isn't fair that her family can come to New York City when my mama will be home alone for Christmas. The crying makes me think of Gran and the big empty space she left in Warren and in my heart, too. And I cry until all of the tears in me are on my pillow and there is nothing left inside.

I lie very quiet on the bed with my face turned away from the door and toward the window. I lie that way for a long time.

Outside the room, I hear footsteps and people going past. And then I hear the sound I am dreading beyond dread. The door opens and Miss Priss comes in.

'Casey?' she says. Her voice is like a rusty nail on a rock.

I keep my mouth shut tight.

She sighs and I can hear her rolling her eyes at me, which makes me grind my teeth.

'I brought you a sandwich,' she says. But I am still zipped up tight.

'Fine, be that way,' she says, and the plate goes down with a clatter. I can feel my stomach folding in on itself, but I wouldn't touch that sandwich if it was the last food on earth.

The other bed creaks and the covers crease and rustle, but I still don't move. The room is quiet. But it is a heavy quiet, like the air in Warren when a big storm is brewing. That quiet sits for a long time, and then it breaks.

My stomach growls like thunder and Miss Priss says, 'Just eat the sandwich. I don't want to listen to your sorry stomach all night.'

'I don't want it,' I say. My voice is ugly, sticking and stretching in my throat.

'Why are you like that? Why are you always so prickly to me? It's just a sandwich.'

'I don't want your sandwich,' I say. And as I say it I know I am being a baby, but I can't stop.

'What is your problem with me, Casey Quinn? I was just trying to be nice because you looked upset. I've been trying to be nice since we moved here.' Her voice sounds hurt, and that makes me angry because what right does she have to be upset with me?

I sit up on my bed so fast my head spins. 'It's a little late to be nice to me now. You were horrible to me in Warren, so why should I be your friend now, just 'cause you don't have all your pinky-pink ballet bees anymore?'

She hugs her knees to her chest. 'I know,' she says, soft and quiet. 'But you made me so mad, always acting like you were better than me.'

I laugh, a mean sound at the back of my throat. '*Me* acting better than *you*? I wasn't always showing off a new dress, or toy, or anything my father bought me. I didn't trip you in the cafeteria, or tell you that you smelled bad.' I can feel all the hatefulness pouring out of my mouth, lemon and vinegar over my tongue.

'I'm sorry I was mean to you,' Miss Priss says, swinging her feet onto the floor and standing up. Her words shock me as much as a slap in the face. 'I know I was horrible, and I'm trying to make it up. Can't you see that? But you've been just as bad to me since we moved here. You never talk to me, and you ignore me at school at lunch . . .' Her voice cracks and I can feel myself going soft, and it makes me so mad at myself because I am not gonna feel sorry for that stuck-up Miss Priss. Not ever.

'I'm not the one bragging about my parents coming to

visit and every little thing we're gonna do together.'

It's the only thing left I can think of to say, but the words taste bitter.

'I'm not bragging. I'm just excited. You'd be excited too if your mom was coming.'

'Well, she's not,' I say as loud as I dare.

'She is,' Miss Priss says.

'She is not!'

'She is, Casey! She's coming in the car with my mom and dad. I would have told you before, but you sulked off and wouldn't talk to me!'

I sit on the bed, my mouth a perfect O. My mama is coming to New York City. I look at Miss Priss staring at me, her hands on her hips. And then I leap.

I have my arms around Miss Priss's neck, but I am not punching or pulling her hair. I jump back dead quick when I realize that I just gave Miss Priss a hug. But I am too happy to care.

'You are so weird,' she says, her hair all ruffled from my squeeze, but even that doesn't worry me.

My mama is coming to New York City for Christmas. My mama is gonna see me dance!

Chapter Thirty-Two

I can't sleep a wink.

Tomorrow is dress rehearsal.

Tomorrow is the day Mama is coming, late at night 'cause she's driving all day with the Ryders.

My heart has run away to play in the fresh fall of snow and my mind is racing with everything I want to do.

Morning creeps up slow and steady, and I can almost hear the sky changing colors as the sun gets closer. I sit in the windowsill, watching as the frosty patterns light up. They look like diamonds sparkling in the orange morning light. I never got to see them when I had to get up for school, but now that it's Christmas break I can sleep in and watch the sun. Dance class starts earlier, 'cause Miss Martha says we all need the practice. But I don't mind, not one bit. Dance is why I came to New York City, and I could dance happy all day long.

After class, Miss Martha tells me to put on my coat and meet her downstairs. I bundle up quick and race outside, two steps at a time, and see her hail a taxi with one beautiful flick of the wrist.

She holds open the yellow door.

'Well? What are you waiting for? Get in,' she says.

The inside of the taxi is dark and warm, and it smells like some sort of exotic spice. I imagine this is what frankincense or myrrh must smell like, and it fills me up with Christmas. I shuffle across the seat to make room as Miss Martha slides in next to me like a ship sailing in from sea. She tells the driver to take us to the Imperial Theater, and the taxi starts to move.

I press my nose to the window, staring at the lights as they fly past. The faces of other people riding in the back of other taxis are like a million moving pictures, and I want to watch every one.

'You've done well, Casey,' Miss Martha says. 'You are really dancing the Maid now. I'm very pleased with you.'

Miss Martha is never free with her praise, and her words make my heart flutter inside my chest, stirring up my middle and making me feel all dizzy inside.

'My mama is coming to watch me dance,' I say, like this

explains everything. And in a way, it does. The thought of Mama in New York City makes my muscles feel strong and full of jump.

'Is this the first time she'll see you perform?'

I nod. Mama's been watching me dance all of my life, but not like this. Not on a grand stage with red velvet curtains.

'She's coming tonight, after rehearsal.' I whisper the words like they are a secret.

Miss Martha's face is very steady and still, and it is hard to tell what she is thinking, but I believe she is happy for me. I smile at her and then, when she looks away, I stare out the window at the bright neon city drifting by. Miss Martha has done so much for me, and I think I will dance better than ever and that will be the best way to say thank you.

It is dark outside when the taxi pulls up outside of the theater. The Imperial is lit up like a Christmas tree. I tip my head back and look up. Above me, written in white round lightbulbs in letters that must be as tall as me, is: 'Martha Graham and Company'. It ain't exactly my name in lights, but it is close enough. Miss Martha doesn't look up. She sweeps past me and I follow her into the theater.

The rest of the Company is already there, stretching and jumping on the stage. They see me coming in with

Miss Martha and think I am just a teacher's pet, but I am too stuffed full of wonder to worry. My name is in lights and my mama is gonna see it.

It is dress rehearsal, so everything must be just like a real show. The front of the theater is full of musicians, and the sound of them tuning their instruments plays along as we warm up. Each note makes a different part of me twitch and itch as I stretch alongside everyone else.

In the dressing room, our costumes are laid out. I hold up the plain white leotard with its long draped skirt in front of me. As I put it on I can feel my heart beat in my fingers and toes. There is a long mirror surrounded by lights, and I walk over to it slowly. I look different. The other dancers are putting on makeup. I look closely at my face. I've never worn lipstick before, not really, but I pick up a tube and run it gently over my lips. A different face looks back at me. A face that looks like my mama. When I see this, me and my reflection smile.

It is time to begin.

Miss Martha waves us to the wings on either side of the stage. We stumble and bump in the dark. The red velvet curtains close and we take our places on the stage, feeling our way to the right space even though it is hard to see. Everything is painted black, and it feels like I am walking with my eyes closed. The air is full of energy and nerves, like the sky before a storm.

The curtain and the music rise together, and Miss Martha starts the dance. Her body is full of music. I watch her in awe. Then I am dancing with her, leaping so high I could brush the lights with my fingertips.

And then I blink and my part is over. I step, graceful in my white dress, back into the shadows, and disappear off-stage.

I stand silent and tall with my back to the wall, watching the rest of the Company perform. I can't see Miss Martha from where I am standing, but I can see the other dancers moving through the space behind her. They swirl and soar, their strong legs digging down into the floor and pushing way up high.

And then everything stops, sudden and hard. One moment the dancers are flying across the stage, and then they're still. The music stops, too. The sudden silence is so loud it makes my ears buzz. The look on everyone's faces makes my knees tremble. Their mouths perfect 'O's, their faces white with worry.

I step forward, my heart drum-rolling as I twist my head around the edge of the curtain. The stage lights are sharp and bright, making my eyes sting, and I blink and step forward with my arm up in the air like a shield. I have a bad feeling inside.

Miss Martha is on the floor, all crumpled like a ragdoll. Time freezes.

For a second I think she is dead. But then she moves and I breathe again, a sigh of relief as big as the ocean.

Someone runs up out of the darkness where the theater seats are, and hands Miss Martha a bag of ice.

'Are you all right?'

'Do I look all right?' Miss Martha is mad snarling, like she is a raccoon caught in a trap. Her eyes are wild and no one is getting too close. But from where I'm standing I can see she's hurt bad. Her ankle is swollen up double its normal size, and the skin is all angry purple and red.

People are whispering about sending for a doctor, but Miss Martha is having none of that.

'I'm fine,' she snaps. 'Just get me a chair.'

But no one believes her. Someone disappears to the front of the theater to call a doctor, and the rest of us stare at Miss Martha, wishing there was something we could do.

Miss Martha looks at us and I know what she is thinking, that she doesn't want us all staring and pitying her. Her mouth is all thin and determined, and she tries to stand up, but the ankle is having none of that and down she goes again. My heart feels like it is splitting in two, and when Miss Martha looks at me, it shatters.

We sit there silent for what seems like forever, Miss Martha refusing to talk, and everyone else too scared to say a word. Then there are more footsteps in the darkness and a doctor arrives, tsking and tutting.

'Now, young lady, let's have a look at that ankle,' he says, and Miss Martha practically growls.

'Who are you calling "young lady"? I am fine. I just need to let it rest for a minute.'

The doctor doesn't pay no mind to Miss Martha saying she is fine. He hums and haws and pokes at her ankle, making Miss Martha wince. Finally, he stands up.

'I'm afraid it is a rather serious sprain, Miss Graham,' he says. 'You're not going to be able to dance on that for some time.'

Miss Martha's face is whiter than white, but she doesn't say a word.

The doctor calls a taxi to take Miss Martha home. Her face is frozen, like she is wearing a mask of herself. Helen gets up to give Miss Martha her shoulder, but Miss Martha is having none of that. 'Don't touch me,' she snaps at Helen, swatting her away like a bottle fly. The whole room flinches.

'You should let someone see you home,' the doctor

says. 'At least to carry your bag.' He says it kind, but he doesn't understand what has happened. Not really.

'Casey,' Miss Martha says, and I jump in my skin and look side to side, then I step forward. 'Get my things.'

I nod but I don't offer any other help, because Miss Martha doesn't want any.

I am down in the dark bit of the theater, my eyes all dazzled with leftover lights. I feel a hand on my arm and I spin around in the darkness.

'Don't let her cancel the show,' a voice says. I think it is Steven, but I'm not sure, as he's never seen fit to talk to me till now. But I don't have the time for being cross. Or the stomach.

'Cancel the show?' I say.

'If she can't be in it, she'll cancel it,' he whispers. His voice is husky and harsh. 'She needs to let someone else dance her part. Edith.'

The doctor and Miss Martha are waiting for me at the lobby door. I can see them framed in the yellow rectangle of light, and I pull my arm away.

'Promise me you'll try,' he says.

'I'll try,' I say, and then I am racing up the aisle toward Miss Martha and the doctor, Miss Martha's coat and bags heavy in my arms.

I take one last look at the Company behind me. They

stand together like they are huddling against the cold. They look so worried and suddenly I am worried, too. What if Miss Martha does cancel the show? What will I tell my mama? It feels like my dreams are dripping down the drain, and I won't let that happen. I wave with one hand at the Company, a soldier's wave, like a salute. Then I am out the door.

Chapter Thirty-Three

My second ride in a taxi is not as good as my first.

I sit on the corner of my seat, trying not to take up any room at all and definitely trying not to touch Miss Martha, who sits in the corner like she is made of stone, while the doctor tells me about the importance of ice on a sprain.

'You'll have to get her a fresh pack once we get her home, and then she needs plenty of rest.'

I nod but I'm hardly listening. I can still feel Steven's squeeze on my arm, like it's reminding me what I've got to do.

The taxi pulls to a stop outside a tall brown building and I hop out, feet splashing in the slush and arms full of stuff, and race round to open the door for Miss Martha.

She slides out, and the doctor helps her up the steps.

'Here, take her keys and get everything opened up. Find a chair and a footstool so Miss Graham can put her foot up.' The doctor gives orders and I jump to obey, running on ahead. It is warm inside and I find the light switch quickly.

I walk down the hall, and open doors until I find the living room. There's a large chair there, and I put a footstool in front of it and wait. The doctor and Miss Martha hobble through the door. The doctor helps her into the chair, then he lifts her ankle gently onto the stool.

'A pillow.' He snaps his fingers, and I hand him one.

Miss Martha's ankle looks so sore and swollen it makes my eyes sting, but Miss Martha doesn't make a sound and she certainly doesn't speak to the doctor, because she has no words for someone like him.

'You need to keep that ankle elevated and ice it for twenty minutes every other hour. I'll send a nurse with some crutches for you in the morning. For now just try to get some rest.'

He puts his hat back on and hands me an empty ice bag from his case. Then he tips his hat to us and leaves. The door clicks behind him and I am alone with Miss Martha.

I stand very still because it's like being in a cage with a tiger. Miss Martha doesn't say a word, but the room is throbbing with pain. Not from her ankle, but from not dancing.

I don't know what to say, because nothing is gonna make that hurt go away, so I walk quiet as a mouse into the kitchen to look for ice. I get a block out of the bottom of the freezer. It is heavy, and I balance it against my chest until I can tip it into the sink. The sides are slick from where it is starting to melt. There is an ice pick in the drawer by the sink. I start to chip away at the block. It is loud work, and I wince and worry about annoying Miss Martha. But she needs the ice and I need to chip it, so I take a deep breath and try to do it as fast and quiet as possible.

I am all nerves because I know what I need to do. I need to ask Miss Martha not to cancel the show, to let Edith dance her part. And I feel low inside, because it will be like stabbing Miss Martha in the back. But I have to do it just the same.

I fill the ice bag with the chips in the sink and screw the lid on tight. Miss Martha is still a statue in her chair. She stirs oh-so-slightly when I put the ice on her ankle. She turns her eyes on me, slow, as if just remembering I am there. She looks at me for a long time and I let her look, because what else can I do?

'Bring me a drink,' she says after ages. 'There is a bottle in the freezer.'

I nod and move sharpish to the kitchen. In the freezer I find a clear bottle with strange writing on it that I can't recognize. It is so cold my fingers stick to the side as I take it out. I climb up on the counter and look for a glass. The cabinets are full of sparkling cut crystal, and I take down one glass, hugging it carefully to my chest. It looks like a snowflake.

I bring Miss Martha the glass and the bottle, and watch as she pours the thick, clear liquid and takes a long sip. The room is quiet. Miss Martha stares past me. I can't read her face at all. My voice is sticky like molasses, but I make myself say the words.

'Are you going to cancel the show?'

Miss Martha looks at me like I am a bug on her clean white carpet.

'I can't dance. How can there be a show if I can't dance?'

She raises her eyebrows at me, like a challenge, like she knows what I am going to say and she is daring me to say it. I swallow hard and hold onto the arm of the sofa to keep me standing up straight.

'Couldn't someone else dance your part?' I say.

I duck down at the same time, and the crystal glass goes flying over my head.

'Someone else?' she hollers at me. 'Someone else!' Her

eyes could light me on fire they glare so hot. 'No one else can dance that part. I choreographed it for me. It is my dance!' She bangs on her chest with an open hand, making a hollow slapping sound that drowns out my drumming heart.

I walk real slow to where the glass hit the wall and pick it up. It smells of strong liquor, as strong as the sherry Mrs Everton keeps hidden behind the sewing set in the kitchen. The glass isn't broken, or even cracked, so I hand it back to Miss Martha. She grabs my wrist. Her red nails look like claws.

'Do you think you can dance my part? Is that what you want?'

I try to pull my arm away but Miss Martha just grabs on tighter.

'You couldn't dance that role. You don't know it, and even if you did you couldn't *dance* it.' She spits out the word 'dance' like she can't even bear to say it while I'm in the same room.

'I know,' I say, softly, trying to be brave. 'But Edith could.'

Miss Martha's face goes from white to near see-through.

'Edith?' she says, like she doesn't even see me there at all. Her eyes are far away, and then suddenly they focus.

'You did this to me,' she says. 'I've seen you, plotting. You've been waiting. You and her. Well, you can't. I'm Martha Graham.' She's shouting now and I back away, out of range of her claws. 'There is no dance without Martha Graham. It's my name on that marquee. Martha Graham, not Edith White. Not Casey Quinn.'

'Yes, but it's still your dance. You made it,' I say. Miss Martha is angry, but I can see now that she is also scared. Scared that someone is taking the dance away from her. Scared just like the rest of us.

Miss Martha makes a sound like someone falling off a cliff, and pounds her fists on the chair cushions so hard it must hurt. I stand firm, my feet planted on the carpet like they are growing roots. And all at once Miss Martha stops screaming and pours herself another drink. She sips and sighs and looks at me. 'Everyone is betraying me. Edith. You. Even my own body.'

I don't know what to say and so I say nothing at all, which is what Gran said made her a wise woman. *Know when to keep your mouth shut, Casey*, she would say, and I think it works.

Miss Martha sighs. 'People say I am too old to dance. That I am past my prime. Is that what you think?'

I shake my head no, and Miss Martha sighs the world.

'Then why do you tell me Edith can dance my part?'

'Because you hurt your ankle and you can't dance tomorrow. It doesn't mean you can't ever dance again.'

Miss Martha's lips move. It is a ghost of a smile, and to me it is sadder than all the crying in the world.

'Go home, Casey. Go see your mother.'

I start because I forgot how late it is, and then I look at Miss Martha because I don't want to leave her alone.

'I'll be fine,' she says, sipping her drink.

I put on my coat, fast and slow, part of me rushing for Mama and another part watching Miss Martha.

'Casey?' Miss Martha makes her voice a question, and I snap to attention like a soldier.

'Bring the phone to me before you go. It's not a promise, but I will think about it,' she says.

I nod and try not to smile, as I know it will vex her. I put the phone on the table next to her, carefully tucking the long cord around the table leg so she won't trip if she gets up.

'I'll see you tomorrow,' I say.

Miss Martha doesn't answer me.

It takes me a long time to get back to Mrs Everton's. My feet are frozen through by the time I open the door, and I stomp them down on the tiles in the little entryway, shivering and shaking as I take off my coat.

I shudder my way into the kitchen, hoping Mrs Everton has left something hot on the stove so I can eat and warm myself by the gas burner. I open the door and I stop solid. Because there is my mama. Sitting at Mrs Everton's kitchen table like we are back in Warren and I just got home from school. But she isn't alone. Steven is sitting with her and Helen and, it seems, Miss Martha's whole Company, crammed into Mrs Everton's postage-stamp kitchen, drinking cups of hot black coffee and wearing their worry on their faces. But all I care about is Mama.

We are on our feet together, and I wrap my arms around her middle and squeeze her with all my might to make sure it is really true. That she is here in New York City with me. Mama squeezes back. It takes my breath away and I don't care who is watching.

'I missed you!' I say. I just didn't know how much.

'I missed you, too.' Mama's voice is fierce and strong, and we hug in the quiet kitchen until my arms feel weak. I give one last squeeze and let go, looking up at Mama's face and smiling. She looks good, my mama. Like the sun is shining out of her skin. I grin until I feel like my cheeks might fall off. She's wearing a new dress, blue like cornflowers, and a matching hat. She looks like she belongs in the City.

As we walk back to the table I can see the worry all over

Steven. He's not interested in me and my mama. He wants to know about Miss Martha.

'What did she say?' he asks as we sit down, and I want him to go away because he is ruining my moment with Mama.

'She said she'd think about it,' I say, and try not to remember the hurt on Miss Martha's face.

'Don't worry,' Mama squeezes my hand, 'Casey could convince a rock to roll uphill.'

Steven doesn't look like he believes her. He opens his mouth and the questions pour out like rain, and I sit listening, wishing for an umbrella.

I am saved when Mrs Everton walks in, her hair hidden in her rollers and her face smeared white with cold cream. She stares at us, and then at the clock, and then at us again. And then she opens her mouth.

'Out!' she squawks. 'Out. Out. Out. This is a respectable boarding house and I will not have my kitchen full of unannounced guests at all hours of the night.'

Steven and his questions are no match for Mrs Everton. She even picks up a broom to shoo them out the door. 'Theater people,' she says as she huffs and puffs, sweeping Miss Martha's dancers out of the hall and onto the street. Mama looks at me with a twinkle in her eye. She puts her fingers to her lips and we sneak like two mice up the stairs.

Miss Priss is staying with her parents at The Ritz where the bathtubs are so big you can swim laps in them, but I don't care 'cause it means Mama and I have the room to ourselves. My chest is so full of my heart I can't speak. I have a million things I want to say, but nothing will come out of my mouth. Mama sits on the bed and rubs her shoulders.

'Is it always this cold?' she asks.

I nod. 'You can put a nickel in the heater, but I'm OK,' I say, because New York City is expensive and I don't want Mama to waste her money on me. But Mama doesn't seem to mind. She puts a coin in the heater slot and turns the dial, and then we sit and wait for it to get warm.

'You look good, Casey,' Mama says. 'I think the City agrees with you.'

I smile wide and suddenly I can speak again. I tell Mama about school and Andrea and classes with Miss Martha. I tell her about saving my pennies to go to the pictures and drinking hot coffee at the cafe. Mama tells me about Warren, and I am so thirsty for news of home that I drink up every word. She is painting again and a woman from Charleston has put her paintings in a gallery.

'Someone even bought one. For ten dollars!' Mama whispers like she can hardly believe it. It's like my mama has grown younger since I've seen her. She is shining like a star and it makes me wish Gran could see her. That Gran could see both of us sitting side by side at Mrs Everton's Boarding House for Young Ladies. But then I think, of course she can see us, my gran. And the thought of her fills me up with so much joy that I have to hug Mama all over again.

Chapter Thirty-Four

We must go to bed at some point, because in the morning I wake up with a jolt and look all around. It isn't a dream. Mama is there, sleeping in Miss Priss's bed.

I itch and twitch out from under the covers and climb in with Mama, whose eyes open so fast I think she wasn't really asleep at all.

'Your feet are like *ice*, Casey!' she says.

It is early morning, but I get up anyway. Mama is so cold she gets dressed like a ghost under the covers. I am full bursting with all of the things I want to show her, and I can't move fast enough. I am into my clothes in one leap, and then into my shoes, dancing by the door with my feet tapping *hurry up, Mama* on the bare wooden boards.

We sneak down the stairs quiet as can be, and Mama makes porridge with milk. It tastes so much like home I can't help smiling. Then it is all bundle and go because we have everything to do.

The air outside is cold and crisp, but I feel warm inside from Mama's porridge and the heat of holding Mama's hand.

There is someone sitting on Mrs Everton's stone front steps and I stop because that someone is wearing a purple beret. It is Edith. She turns as my feet crunch the snow. Her cheeks and nose are both red, but she is smiling as she stands up to say hello.

'You did it, Casey,' she says, and I am a mirror, smiling right back at her. Mama hugs my shoulder tight to her side.

'You need to come to the Imperial early so we can all practice together before the show. OK?'

I nod. Nothing in this whole world would stop me from being there.

Edith says goodbye and walks up the snowy street. I wave and wave until she is just a purple speck in the crowd. Then I grab my mama's hand and we are off.

Mama's face is all up up up, looking high into the sky at the buildings we walk by. I work hard weaving us in and out of the New Yorkers, who don't have time to wonder at their City and only look down at the street beneath their feet.

Andrea is waiting for us at the cafe, sitting at the counter and saving two seats for us.

'It's so nice to meet you, Andrea,' Mama says. 'Casey's told me all about you.'

'Nice to meet you, too. What are you going to do today?' Andrea asks me.

'We're gonna see everything.' I say. I am bubbling over and can hardly sit still, spinning and shifting on my stool as I sip hot coffee. 'We'll go to Times Square, and we'll see the Christmas tree in Rockefeller Center, and go for a carriage ride in Central Park, and see the Empire State Building and—'

Mama laughs and says, 'Calm down, Casey, we have all morning.'

'I know, but I want to show you everything!' I say. I want to press all of New York into a little ball so I can give it to my mama.

'I've got some extra tickets for the matinée today,' Andrea says, 'if you want to come see it.'

'Of course!' I say. 'Andrea's a snowflake and she's the best of all of them,' I say to Mama, as Andrea hands me two tickets.

'And since we're doing a matinée today we have

tonight off, so I can come see your show!'

I am so full of joy I spin on the spot, three whole turns without a wobble in sight. Andrea laughs, but it's a happy laugh and it makes me want to spin all over again. But instead I wrap my arms around Andrea and squeeze. 'You can sit with my mom. I'm so happy you're coming!'

Mama and Andrea agree to meet outside the theater before the show. Then Andrea looks at the diner clock.

'Well, I gotta run or I'll be late for curtain. I'll see you later!'

Mama and I both wish her good luck. Andrea runs out the door, waving goodbye, and then stops sudden and sticks her head back inside.

'I forgot. My sister says if you still want to come, you are both very welcome to have Christmas morning with us. As long as you're happy for Casey to cook, Mrs Quinn.' She grins.

I look at Mama and I know what she's thinking. That we'll cook together. And the thought of being in the kitchen with my mama makes me glow. Mama and I agree, and then Andrea is running down the street.

I take Mama to Central Park to show her the garden in the middle of the city. There are rows and rows of carriages waiting to take us for a ride and we choose one with a beautiful black horse.

The driver gives us a warm blanket to tuck around our legs, and then we are off. The bells on the horse's halter jingle-jangle as we trot through the park, past the frozen pond full of people ice skating and then out of the trees to where we can see the Empire State Building shining in the morning sun like a giant rocket ship reaching into the sky. Mama's mouth is open wide and I am full of pride because I live here.

At noon, the carriage drops us off in front of the main door of the theater, which has a big sign over the top that says 'The Nutcracker'. The driver helps Mama down and then reaches up his hand to steady me as I jump out, but I don't need steadying. Nothing in the world could knock me over. I am not walking, I am flying!

I'm so happy I have to squeeze Mama all over again to let some of the joy come out. Mama is smiling a secret smile when I look up at her. 'What?' I say, but she won't tell me and bundles us into the theater without another word.

Inside, the theater is nearly as grand as the Imperial. There are painted ceilings and rich red carpets and gold molding like we are inside a castle. A man in a blue and gold jacket looks at our tickets, and we follow his pointing finger toward a spiraling staircase up to the balcony. The stage seems very small below us, and I lean forward to get a better look, Mama gripping onto my jacket 'cause she's worried I might fall over the edge. Then the lights go low and the music starts. I sit on my hands and try and keep still.

The ballet is beautiful, all bright colors and presents around a giant Christmas tree that grows like magic in the night. The story is written in the program and some people keep reading along with the dance, but I don't need to. I can read the dance itself, thank you very much, plain as the words on a page.

Miss Priss is all spoiled golden curls, but I can't say she's a bad dancer. She whirls and turns like she was born on stage, as I wait for Andrea to appear. And then there she is, all frosty silver in her costume, flying across the stage just like a snowflake sparkling in the sun. She is beautiful and my heart leaps alongside her. My arms wiggle and I sit down firm on my fingers to stop them from waving along with the music.

I look at Mama out of the corner of my eye. The light from the stage is beautiful on her face, and she is smiling honest and true. I reach out and take her hand in the darkness, and she squeezes my fingers. So we sit, side by side, watching the ballet, and I think we are both dancing along with it in our hearts.

When the ballet is over, Mama walks with me down

the street to the Imperial Theater.

'Look,' I say, pointing up at the lights. 'It says "*Martha Graham and Company*". And I am in the Company.' I look at Mama looking at the sign and my heart gets so big it squeezes tears out of my eyes. Mama looks and looks at that sign.

'I wish Gran was here,' I say quiet and small, but Mama hears me. She wraps her arm around my shoulder.

'I do, too,' she says. 'But she knew you, Casey. She always believed in you. She knew you were going to do big things and here you are, proving her right. I know she would be very proud of you.'

My heart gets even bigger, impossibly big, and my eyes are sparkling cold where the tears are freezing on my eyelashes.

'And I am very proud of you, too.'

I hug Mama fierce and look up at her.

'Will you be OK?' I ask, because New York City is a big place and I am suddenly worried about leaving her alone. But Mama just laughs.

'I'm a grown woman, Casey Quinn. I will be just fine. Now you go in and get ready. I will see you on that stage. OK?'

I have no words.

'OK, then. Scoot!'

Mama gives me one last hug and then she pushes me through the door into the theater. I walk quickly across the lobby and open the door to the theater itself. I take one last look over my shoulder. Mama is still there, looking up at my name in lights, her breath puffing out like smoke and her cheeks rosy from the cold winter air. Then I dash through the door into the theater for the last rehearsal before the show.

Chapter Thirty-Five

Rehearsal goes fast, fast, fast, like sand slipping through my fingers. My stomach is a dancer all by itself, twisting and turning in my middle and making me feel green and dizzy. I blink and we are done. Then I am sitting in a chair while Edith puts greasepaint on my face and scowls at me to sit still.

'Do you think she'll come?' I say, around a tube of lipstick. Edith looks daggers at me.

'I told you to hold still,' she says. Her face is already painted white like Miss Martha's, but Miss Martha is not here.

'Sorry,' I say, but I can't help asking the question again.

Edith sighs. 'I don't think so. Now hold still.'

I open my mouth like an O and hold as still as I can

manage. I wish Miss Martha *was* here, but when I remember how she looked when I asked her to let Edith dance her part, I know she won't come. It would hurt too much.

'There.' Edith is finished. I leap off the chair. My legs are coiled with spring. I look in the mirror and smile. Edith does my makeup much better than I do.

Backstage the air is so thick I feel I could run my fingers through it like water. Everyone is moving and stretching, but no one is talking. It is like everyone is inside their own little space.

The clock on the wall says it is still twenty minutes to the show. I feel like my skin has been stripped off and all of my nerves are right there on the surface. I tiptoe to the stage door and slip inside. The curtains are closed, but I can hear the audience on the other side like a live animal. A low bubbling sound that makes my insides trill.

I walk up to the curtain slow and soft. The fabric is thick between my fingers, and it is heavy, too. I give a little pull and a slice of light falls across my feet. I put my eye up to the gap and peek out. I think maybe I will be able to see Mama and Andrea, but I don't. All I see are people. Hundreds and hundreds of them, and my heart starts to beat hard. I let the curtain fall, and step back into the darkness.

My head is spinning, and I rest it against the wall and

close my eyes. I am scared. What if I fall, or forget my steps, or am just plain no good? What if they don't like me? What if I let everyone down? The worry worm wraps itself tight around my middle, making me want to curl up into the floor. But I don't. I stand up straight, because when did I ever let being scared stop me before? Not once, not ever. And I ain't gonna start letting that happen now.

I shift my weight from foot to foot because the moving helps somehow. I close my eyes and sway in the darkness. I am home in Warren, dancing on the sidewalk, not caring who sees me, because I am Casey Quinn and I was born to dance.

'There you are! I told you not to wander off.' Edith has my shoulder in the dark. And because we are in the dark, I am brave enough to tell the truth.

'I'm scared,' I say.

'That's OK, we're all a little scared. It's opening night,' she says. 'I'd be worried if you weren't. The important thing is not to let it show.'

I nod, even though I know she can't see me.

'We're going to start now. Are you ready?'

I whisper, 'Yes.'

I can hear the rest of the Company padding onto the stage and the low, whining sound of the orchestra starting to warm up, like crickets chirping in the night. And I am ready.

I find my place on the stage and stand in the dark, letting the music fill me to the brim from the other side of the curtain until I am almost overflowing. I can feel the other dancers around me, shimmying and stretching and settling into their skin. I can feel them like they are my fingers and I know exactly where they are. And when I think hard, I can feel my mama somewhere out in the audience, and Andrea, too. And somewhere out there, or maybe somewhere inside of me, I can feel my gran.

The music swells up and the curtains lift. Lights hit me bright as dawn.

And we dance.

Edith starts, moving across the stage like she is a fire. My heart pounds as loud as the drums, but I let go and listen. I have my reason to dance, and when I move I move every part of my body, dancing down to my fingertips. Not just moving my arms as they carve the air on the stage, but moving them with purpose, like I am carving all the air in the whole theater. In the whole world.

I can feel Edith dancing behind me and we carve the space together, weaving around each other like starlings cartwheeling through the evening sky.

I leap high, pushing out of the floor and tipping my

head back to the ceiling. I am breaking free of gravity. Andrea is in the audience so I leap higher. Higher again for my mama. And even higher because Gran is out there watching, too. And I leap highest of all for me, because I am here. Casey Quinn, dancing on a real New York City stage, shining as bright as the footlights. I leap with everything that took me out of South Carolina, high as the clouds above the Empire State Building. And I land without a sound, still and solid and in control. My lungs are burning but I hold statue still, eyes wide open until the music shifts again and I step offstage.

From backstage in the wings I watch as Edith leaps and falls. And as the other dancers move with her, I do, too. Swinging and swaying and folding at the middle. Edith leaps high, and it makes my heart soar. I feel guilty for thinking it, but she's amazing. I never saw Miss Martha dance like that. Now I understand why she couldn't come.

Then Helen flies fierce across the stage as Joan the Warrior, fighting with gravity to stop holding her down, and it's my turn again.

Back onstage, I'm rising and falling to the earth as Joan is martyred. I fold and fall to the floor without a sound, sending my energy out into the theater, and the sorrow makes me think of Miss Martha, who made the dance but cannot bear to watch it. I rise and fall again, harder, wishing I could bring it back to her. Eventually the dance becomes slower and slower until everyone falls for the last time.

The curtain drops, but I stay perfectly still like I am under a spell. I feel everything all at once, the floor on my chest and my cheek, the air against my back, the smell of warm greasepaint under the hot theater lights. My heart aches with sadness for Miss Martha and the joy of dancing in New York City for my mama. I feel everything, but I also feel empty, like maybe all of these things are draining out of me, leaving me light as a feather.

'Get up, Casey!' Edith pulls me to my feet. 'Time to take a bow.'

I let her pull me into line with the other dancers. She nods to someone invisible in the wings and the rich red curtains rise again.

The lights and the sound wash over me like waves, and Edith has to tug me forward when the company steps one-two-three in front of the curtain. The audience is full of faces and hands clapping like a million leaves fluttering in the wind.

I look for Mama and Andrea but I still can't find them in the crowd. I can't believe how many people came to see us.

Edith starts the bow and I follow her, bending low

from the waist. I smile wide as wide can be. Helen steps forward and there are great cheers, and for Steven, too. Then it is my turn.

I step forward and my senses feel all wobbly with fear and joy. For a moment, I worry that they will stop clapping. That they will look at my chicken legs and ask, *Who let this awkward girl on stage?* But they don't. They clap loud as ever. And then I see Mama and Andrea standing up and cheering me on. Andrea is holding a bunch of flowers and Mama has her hands high over her head. I bow, pulling myself back up taller than before, the way Miss Martha taught me. I bow so my whole body says *Thank You* better than I could ever say it in words.

They are clapping for me and I can't hardly believe it is true. Not just Mama and Andrea, but the whole audience clapping and cheering because they liked watching me dance.

I step back into the line, and Edith moves forward full of power and grace, and the clapping gets even louder, and I clap too because we couldn't have done it without her.

I look at Edith and then I look at the audience cheering, and I feel very proud, but something else, too. A kind of hungry, I think. I made it all the way to New York City and I danced on a New York City stage. But dreams don't just come true, not really. They come true, and then they get bigger. I'm not just gonna stop dancing 'cause I got this far. Some day I'll dance the lead, and then, some day after that, I'll dance all over America. I'll keep dancing until my name is up in lights all over the world.

My name is Casey Quinn and I am a dancer and I ain't never gonna stop. You hear me? Nope. Not ever!

Acknowledgements

First I would like to thank my tutors and fellow students on the 2005/06 MA programme Writing for Children at the University of Winchester. Specifically, Andrew Melrose and Judy Waite for their guidance while I was working on *Dreamer Ballerina*'s early drafts. Thanks also to fellow student Pien Wensing, the best beta reader a writer could ask for!

Big thanks to my agent, Lindsey Fraser, not only for working tirelessly on finding a home for this book, but also for her advice on the manuscript and on being a writer in general. I would not be here without her.

I've been very lucky to work with a great editorial team at The Chicken House and want to thank them all for their enthusiasm for *Dreamer Ballerina* through countless rewrites and rereads. I'd especially like to thank Imogen Cooper, Nicki Marshall and Rachel Hickman for understanding Casey and how far she could go.

Last, but certainly not least, I couldn't have written this book without the love and support of my family. To my four amazing parents for teaching me that I can do anything I put my mind to. To my siblings Hava, Bayla, Ben and Schuyler for filling my life with stories that I constantly steal for writing purposes. And to my husband Chris for always taking such good care of me. I will never be able to say how much I love you.